# HORSEMASTER

# HORSEMASTER

*Marilyn Singer*

*Atheneum*  New York  1985

**Library of Congress Cataloging in Publication Data**

Singer, Marilyn.
The horsemaster.

"Argo book."
SUMMARY: Jessica dreams of a flying horse, then finds
an old tapestry with the power to summon up her dream
horse, on which she flies away through time and space
to fulfill her destiny in a distant, war-torn land.
[1. Fantasy. 2. Space and time—Fiction. 3. Horses—
Fiction] I. Title.
PZ7.S6172Ho      1985      [Fic]      84-21522
ISBN 0-689-31102-8

Published simultaneously in Canada by
McClelland & Stewart, Ltd.
Composition by Heritage Printers, Charlotte,
North Carolina
Printed and bound by Fairfield Graphics,
Fairfield, Pennsylvania
Designed by Felicia Bond
First Edition

*To Dena Aronson, Andrew Ramer and Joanne Ryder,*
*Horsemasters all.*

# HORSEMASTER

# 1

THE HORSE still dances on the horizon.

She holds out her hand. "Come to me," she says. "Please come this time."

There is a stillness, the kind that hangs in the air when a decision is about to be made. Then the horse tosses his head, and in a moment, he is there by her side.

She mounts easily, strokes his neck. "I will go with you," she says.

He whinnies once. Then the hooves strike the hard ground. The chestnut flanks shine, muscled and strong. The mane whips lightly against her cheek.

"Faster," she whispers. "Faster."

The hooves clatter. The trees, grass blur around them, a dizzy green. A wind rises, whistling through her white gown. It grows colder, but she doesn't care.

"Faster," she whispers again. "Faster."

The hooves make no sound. The sky, so blue it surprises her, meets them. The land is far below. They rip through a cloud. She closes her eyes.

"JESSICA, I'M leaving now."

Clouds all around, blocking the sun.

"Jessica."

Losing speed. The ground swelling steeply upward. Falling.

"Jessica, I'm talking to you."

She gasped, shuddered. Then she opened her eyes. "Am I hurt?" she asked.

"What are you talking about? Of course you're not hurt," her mother snapped. "You must have been dreaming."

"Yes, dreaming," Jessica said, softly, and was immediately sorry.

"What were you dreaming about?" It was not a question; it was a command.

"Something about a horse," Jessica said reluctantly.

"A horse! You've never been on a horse in your life."

Jessica said nothing. She was awake now and looking at her mother with sullen disdain.

"You don't even ride a bike well," her mother said, and laughed.

Jessica remained silent.

"When I was fourteen, I was the best bike rider in town," her mother continued. But when Jessica failed to respond she stopped talking.

"Are you going to work now?" Jessica finally asked.

"Oh damn, now I'm going to be late," her mother said, leaping to the door. "You're always making me late." As she hurried downstairs, she called, "Now you make sure you dress warmly today. There's a can of soup in the cupboard and bread in the bin. And don't you go out!"

"But I'm going back to school tomorrow," Jessica said.

"Tomorrow's tomorrow. Today's today. And you will do as

I say, young lady," her mother yelled up. "And if that Jack shows his face here, don't you dare let him in, you hear?"

Then she slammed the door, and soon Jessica heard the car start up in the driveway.

She shut her eyes, trying to recapture the dream. The horse. It had finally come to her. And she had ridden, no, flown on him.

She had dreamed of him so many times before. The dreams were beautiful, although frustrating, because the horse had refused to approach her. But this time he *had* come. Why had he come? And where had she been going with him? The questions suddenly frightened her as much as the dreams did. For there were other dreams: battles full of shadowy figures; men in patchwork robes walking in a processional; someone—something—shrouded in veils; blood. Sometimes the horse was there, and she would cry to him for help. She'd awake, tangled in the sheets and sweating, with the sick feeling she was dreaming someone else's dreams.

Once, she had tried talking to Jack about the dreams, but it was difficult.

"Did you ever have . . . funny dreams?" she'd begun.

"Funny ha-ha or funny weird?" Jack asked.

"Funny weird."

"Sure, lots of times. Everybody does."

She tried again. "But did you ever feel as if they weren't your dreams? Sort of like you were looking into a mirror and seeing a reflection that looked a lot like you, but wasn't you?"

Jack furrowed his brow. "I don't think so. Do you?"

"Sometimes . . ."

"That is weird. But, then again, everybody has weird dreams. I wouldn't worry about them if I were you."

Not even if you think the dreams are sort of calling you, as though there's something you're supposed to do, she had wanted to say; but she didn't. She couldn't trust even Jack with that confidence. She didn't want him to think she was crazy and refuse to see her again. Then she'd be all alone with her mother.

Suddenly, a handful of stones rattled against her window.

She jumped. And then she giggled at herself and scrambled out of bed to the window.

It was Jack, just as she knew it would be.

She raised her left hand, opened and shut it three times, and then raced down the stairs in her nightgown and bare feet.

"SO, THE coast is clear—the old battle-axe is gone," he said as he followed her into the warm kitchen.

"Yes, thank God. Why'd you cut today?"

"You'll find out. So, how about some hot chocolate, and then we can leave."

"I'm supposed to stay in today."

"Why? You're over the flu, aren't you?"

"Yes, but Mother thinks I might have a relapse."

"Since when do you listen to her?"

"She might be right this time. I still feel kind of weak." She didn't want to tell him that she was afraid today, something she rarely was.

"Why? Because your mother said stay in and good little Jessica always listens to her mother!" he blurted out.

Jessica said nothing, but her face got very white. Damn! Even though it wasn't true—and Jack knew it—his remark struck a nerve.

There was a long silence. Finally, the kettle whistled.

"I'm sorry, Jess," Jack said quietly. "I'm not helping things that way." He patted her hand.

"That's okay," she mumbled, arising and pouring the water from the kettle into mugs and popping cocoa mix in each.

"It's warm today," Jack said. "But you'll need a jacket anyway."

"What for?" Jessica said, settling the mugs down on the table.

"For a motorcycle ride."

"Oh Jack!" Her arm shot out and she spilled her hot chocolate. "Andrew lent it to you!"

"Let's just say I borrowed it," Jack said, and chuckled.

"You mean he doesn't know?" she asked, alarmed.

"No, and he won't find out. Now, how about a ride?"

Jessica looked at him, at his thin, determined face, his dark eyes always so intense and so restless. My friend Jack, she thought, the fifteen-year-old town terror. Lord, how her Mother detested him.

They'd met two years before. Jessica was walking through the park. She rounded a turn in the path and saw a boy, stretched out under a tree, eating a sandwich, his bike propped up against the trunk. An officious attendant was hassling him about ruining the grass. "There is no grass under this tree. Never has been. Grass won't grow in the shade," the boy said. The attendant was insistent. The boy rose slowly to his feet, casually separating the halves of his sandwich as he did so. The attendant turned to go. The boy stuck the gooey bread onto the man's back. By the time the man had noticed, the boy and his bike were already gone.

Jessica had shaken her head and giggled. The boy was gross, but she liked what he'd done. She'd walked on, thinking about how she'd like to tell some people off sometime, when a young starling landed right at her feet. She picked it up and saw its wing hanging limply. "Oh, little guy, what do I do now," she said aloud.

"Let me see it," a voice behind her said curtly.

She jumped, then turned. It was the boy. Without a word, she held out the bird.

"Wing's busted. I might be able to fix it. Let's take it to my house."

He'd wrapped the starling in a handkerchief and laid it gently in the basket behind the bike seat. "Get on," he told Jessica. She climbed onto the handlebars.

At his house, he skillfully set the bird's wing using a popsicle stick and gauze, and it wasn't until he finished that he turned to Jessica and asked her name.

She told him and then said, "You did a good job."

He shrugged. "I can fix anything."

They became friends quickly. Jack saw an anger and a daring

in Jessica that no one else had. He encouraged it, and so Jessica let it grow. Jack's rebelliousness moved in all directions. He managed to infuriate a myriad of people in a myriad of ways—by backtalking or writing cryptic messages on assorted walls, by sabotaging the school's assembly or by beating up a smooth-talking, popular senior who was extorting money from several younger kids. But Jessica's rebelliousness was more focused. She never got into trouble at school. Her willfulness had one mark—her mother. All the silent anger that had built up over the years found its expression in a new, hard defiance. She bathed when her mother said to conserve water, went dirty when her mother told her she looked like a bum. She ignored her mother at the dinner table, stayed out past curfews, spent money intended for food on books or presents for Jack. She knew her gestures were small and petty, but she relished them.

Jack was watching her now. "It's just like flying," he said.

*That's what I'm afraid of*, she thought. *I can't*, she started to say, but instead, that delicious sense of defiance washed over her. *This is a big one; Mom hates motorcycles*, she thought. Shivering a little in excitement, she said, "I'll be ready in five minutes."

As she pulled on her jeans, the feeling of the dream came back to her. The glorious giddiness. The wind-wracked soaring. She could feel herself letting go, giving in to the dream. Then something cold seemed to touch her. A point of light? The tip of a knife? An icy hand? She shuddered as fear welled up in her once more and she thought again of the other dreams. The horse was part of them, too. And suddenly she understood that if she accepted the horse, she had to accept everything. "Leave me alone," she said aloud. "Please go away and leave me alone."

# 2

WHERE I am I cannot tell. It must be the Magus's doing. He said I had to wait. But I did not know it would be so long a waiting.

I wonder if my father and mother wait, too. And Gamesh.

No. Gamesh no longer waits. The Magus said he could do nothing for him. That no one can do anything for him. No one can use the ma-lat to bring things back to life. He talks so often of the ma-lat. "The shadoor, the soldier, the dancer, the thief, all have, all are the ma-lat," he says. But I do not understand him. I could see the ma-lat, like the sun at summer solstice, in my father, my dear father, whom I so grievously failed. And I saw it too in my mother, but dark as the stones in the palace dungeon. I do not want to think on this, but I must. I must remember. If I do not, I fear there will be nothing left of me. I have already lost home and family. And the tapestry. My father's legacy. Gone, and I am to blame. And because of my cowardice, the kingdom may be lost.

I remember the last time I saw my father. I could not sleep. The night pressed down on me like the slab over the Chosen One's cell. I slipped outside to breathe the heavy air. And there he was, astride his horse, Gampura. But his form held no pride, and his face was drawn and sad.

"Father, where are you going?" I cried, startling him, Gampura and his small retinue.

He dismounted. "My dear one, you should not be awake at this hour. I am traveling to the North."

I did not understand. "Why are you going to the North?"

"I must . . . rest," he answered.

"Take me with you. I want to rest too."

His laughter was full of pain. "No, my dear one. You are needed here."

"How?"

Then, as though the great god Kadi himself had whispered into his ear, his face changed. "You must guard the horse."

"Which horse?" I asked. "Gamesh knows all the horses. He can help me."

"No, he does not know this horse," my father replied. Then he said quickly, "Listen carefully to me, my daughter. In my chamber hangs a tapestry. You may have noticed it. I want you to watch it, to guard it. Do not let it fall into evil hands." He touched my cheek.

I understood nothing, but I nodded. Then I embraced him. He kissed the top of my head. "I shall miss you, daughter."

"Will you return soon?" I asked.

"I do not know," he replied. Then, mounting his horse, he and his men rode away.

I turned my head to wipe my tear-filled eyes and glanced up at a narrow window. There, lit by the moonlight, I saw for an instant my mother's face. And on it was a peculiar smile. It frightened me, although I could not tell why.

Ah, I cannot think on this any longer. I will be as patient as stone. I do not know what more to do.

# 3

JESSICA WATCHED as Jack straddled the motorcycle, a large machine lovingly polished by its fastidious owner. With his helmet and goggles and his jacket zipped high to his throat,

Jack looked older and rather dangerous. He handed Jessica a red helmet and grinned broadly when she slipped it on.

"A real Hell's Angel," he said. "Very tough."

But Jessica wasn't feeling very tough.

Jack started the engine, and the machine leaped awake, growling fiercely.

Jessica swallowed hard.

"Climb on," Jack called.

"What would Mother say if she saw me now," she said, to cover her fear.

"What? I can't hear you over this noise. But whatever it is, don't worry," he shouted.

Slowly, she walked over to the bike. She took a deep breath and climbed onto the seat. It was hot from the sun, and it startled the insides of her legs. The vibrations of the motor felt strange: the strainings of some great beast panting for a run.

"Hold on tight," Jack said.

She encircled his waist and pressed against him. His back felt strong. Strong and warm. She drew away.

"Jack, if anyone sees us, we'll be in a mess," she said.

"No one's going to see us. I'll stick to the back roads. Now listen, all you have to do is hold on and lean the same way the bike and I are leaning."

"What do you mean?" she asked.

"Don't worry, you'll understand as soon as we start." And then he slowly maneuvered the motorcycle down the driveway and to the street corner. "Here we go," he yelled.

With a roar, the machine took off down the street. Jessica felt her stomach tighten. As they rounded a corner, the machine leaned to the right so low to the ground that Jessica feared they'd topple over. She breathed sharply, painfully, and squeezed Jack tightly.

"Good, you're doing fine," he called over his shoulder.

Then, she realized she had automatically leaned over when the motorcycle turned the corner, and she silently applauded herself for this small triumph.

They raced through streets sparsely populated with large old houses much like Jessica's and out into the countryside.

Fields appeared, dotted here and there by farms, sprawling or compact, ancient or modern. An old hexagonal barn sprang up and then disappeared just as quickly. A herd of cows seemed to shake their heads disapprovingly at the roaring disturbance that tore past them. A rabbit scuttled across the road, and they narrowly avoided hitting it.

"Oh, no," Jessica gasped, and wondered if they had the right to disturb the animals' peace.

Soon, the tarmac ended, and the road became dirt. Jessica glanced behind and saw the cloud of dust they left in their wake. A small side road appeared, and Jack recklessly ripped down it. The path was lined with oak trees; leaves from low-hanging branches brushed their helmets. I could pull off some acorns, Jessica thought, but she didn't dare let go of Jack.

He pushed up the speed. The trees and grass began to blur. The wind whipped around them.

"I told you it's like flying," he yelled.

And suddenly Jessica's arms relaxed around his waist and she laughed, a loud, long laugh carried away by the wind.

"Like flying," she called back.

But some subtle, teasing voice within her said, "No, not quite, not like in the dream."

They crossed a little iron bridge. The wheels clattered on the slats. The water below was a quick glint of silver. And then, to the left, a ramshackle building suddenly appeared. She felt something clutch at her stomach.

"Stop here!" she yelled, on a sudden impulse.

"What?"

"STOP!"

"Yes ma'am," Jack said, slowing the motorcycle.

He guided it into a space that must have once been a flower garden. But all that was left now was a clump of wild asters. The building was a brick farmhouse, at least sixty or seventy years old. A sign that said EGGS hung crazily from the tiled roof. And near the porch was a trough full of green and stagnant water.

"This is just an old wreck," Jack said. "Nobody and nothing's here anymore."

But Jessica stiffly climbed off the bike and started for the door. She pushed. It opened easily. With a little smile, she stepped inside.

The room must have once been the parlor. One rickety cane chair and a solid, though cracked, sideboard were all that remained of the furniture; these were shrouded in a thick layer of dust. On the window ledge were a cobwebbed row of clay pots that may once have held geraniums. Jessica peered inside them. The soil that remained was hard and bare. She backed away quickly to a corner of the room.

"Very inviting," Jack said from the doorway. "Can we go now?"

Jessica opened her mouth to say, "yes," when her shoulder brushed against something on the wall. She started, looked up.

It was a tapestry, dingy and old, like everything else in the room. And there, in its threads, was woven the starred head of a chestnut horse.

Trembling, she began to brush more dust away. The chest, the mane, the flanks appeared. "It is," she whispered.

"What are you looking at?" Jack sauntered over. "Hey, that's an antique," he said, looking at the tapestry. "Might even be worth something."

But Jessica wasn't listening to him.

"Do you want to take it?" he went on. "I don't think anyone'd care."

Suddenly, the room grew very cold. The dust from the tapestry began to swirl.

She whirled around. "Jack, let's get out of here," she said urgently.

"Okay with me," he answered. "Hey, your teeth are chattering!"

The cold wound about her. The dust rose, a gray column taking shape. "Out . . . of . . . here . . ." she gasped.

As though from a distance she heard Jack say, "Jess, come on!" Then the room began to shine—silver, silver and white. Blinding white. Like ice. Like snow. Like sand. And at the center, a gray column grew arms.

"Jack!" she shrieked.

He grabbed at her wrist. "Outside," he ordered. "You need air."

She took a step backward and lost his hand. The white was all around. And she could see nothing but the gray figure before her. She tried to spin away.

Then it spoke. "Going so soon?" it said.

And she was unable to move.

# 4

WHEN I was but a child—eight or so—there was a time of joy. My father ruled happily, and my mother had not yet chosen the left-handed path. My brother and I played sheshbesh in the courtyard. And Gamesh taught us how to ride. The dancers came often then; the olive harvest was good; and the Horse-master was just a pleasant legend.

Once a year there was the glorious festival of Ma-lat-El-le, where, spinning and singing, we would praise with heart and hand the beauty of our land and its people and the peace that reigned there. We were all one under the eye of Kadi, of Bodar, of Golgon, of all the gods, and we rejoiced in that knowledge. On that day, my father, clad in the breechcloth of a farmer, worked in the fields; my mother, in homespun, winnowed the grain with her countrywomen; and my brother and I ran in the fields, filling our mouths with sweet figs we pulled from the branches and tumbling in the grass with the farmers' children. It was my favorite day of the year, and I welcomed it as much as I shunned and detested the Horse Sacrifice.

But then came the year my mother refused to attend the Ma-lat-El-le, saying it was unseemly for a queen. I could not understand. How could it be unseemly to join at work with our beloved people. I was more than a little shocked in my childish way. My father could not make her go, and it was from that time the rift between them formed and he grew weary of his rule.

And then my mother turned to magic. She tried to teach it to me, but I had no aptitude. Nor did my brother. No, I lie. I had aptitude, but no desire. Or perhaps the desire was hidden, quenched by fear. Oh, if I had practiced, I might have turned my mother from the left-hand path, but I failed her, just as I did my father. I fled my mother's magic. So she practiced alone. Little spells and invocations. I did not dare listen closely; though, at the beginning, they were most likely harmless enough. It was only much later that her path became clear. But by then she had divided the hearts of our people, had guided them along roads they would not otherwise have traveled. When I saw this, I ached for them, but still I did nothing.

And then the Magus came. I little understand this Magus. He is not like the others, although I have seen him put on the patchwork robe. He frightens me. He told me he would help me to safety. I did not know he would take me behind the veil to do so. I did not know he would take me out of time.

# 5

"PLEASE DO not take your leave until we are properly introduced." The voice was soft and mocking.

Jessica blinked. The white had gone. The spinning had stopped. The room was warm once again. Carefully, she flexed her fingers. *I'm alive,* she thought. *I may be crazy, but at least*

*I'm alive.* She blinked once more, and her eyes focused on the figure before her.

He was a dusty little man, brown and wizened, wearing a woven robe of gray and white and a turban. His wide mouth was turned up in a small smile. As she stared at him, he bowed gracefully.

"Did you speak?" she asked, feeling vaguely like Alice in Wonderland.

"That is what one usually does with one's voice, is it not?"

"Oh God, you did speak. What do you want with me? And where's Jack?" she cried.

"Your friend is behind you," the little man said.

Jessica turned on her heel. Jack was indeed there. Frozen. His mouth was fixed in a question; his eyes were turned toward her. But he said nothing and saw nothing.

"Jack!" She shook him. He was not stiff, yet she was unable to move him. She whirled back to the little man. "What have you done to him?"

"Do not worry. Your friend is safe," he replied.

"Then bring him back. Free him!" she ordered.

"I will free him. But not yet. Not until I have answered something of your first question, Jessica."

She started. "You know my name."

He smiled. "Ashtar," he said, bowing once more. "And now you know mine."

"Have I dreamed of you, too?" she asked.

He waved a thin hand with long fingers. "Let us say we dreamed of one another, Jessica."

*I am crazy*, she thought.

"You are perfectly sane," Ashtar said.

"How did you know what I was thinking?" she asked.

"It is not so difficult a feat to master once you understand the ma-lat."

"The what?"

But he merely smiled again and said nothing.

"I don't remember dreaming you, although I remember some awfully scary dreams. And I remember the horse—" She stopped as the memory of what had so recently transpired flooded her mind. "The horse. In the tapestry! You know about it!"

"It is excellent to see a child of your age so interested in ancient art," he replied, gesturing at the tapestry.

"Stop laughing at me!" she snapped.

"I apologize," Ashtar said gravely. After a pause, he said. "Yes. I know about the horse. And about the tapestry. It has an interesting story behind it. Shall you hear it?"

"I don't know . . . I . . ."

"It is a good story. I will tell it to you over cocoa. That is what American children imbibe, is it not?" he asked, a trace of laughter returning to his voice.

"I don't want any."

"Then, perhaps tea, my country's beverage?" He motioned to the sideboard, now laden with a fat-bellied teapot and two painted cups.

"Please. I want to go home now. So, if you'll free my friend . . ." To Jessica's disgust, her voice had taken on a wheedling tone.

He ignored her and set before them the steaming and fragrant brew. "Shabash! To your health," he said, and as he waited for her to take the first sip before partaking of his cupful, she had little choice but to drink.

"The tapestry is very old. It comes from a distant time and a distant place. It was woven as a gift for a very grand shadoor or king, as your people might put it. It is of very fine workmanship, is it not?"

"I guess so," she mumbled.

"The tapestry holds many secrets and many powers. There was a spell woven into it by a great magus, a magician. Because of this spell, the shadoor's own wife turned against him and the tapestry slipped from his hands."

Jessica shuddered and put up her hand as if to stop him.

"But you do not need to know of the spell yet," he continued. "You need only know that the tapestry is here, now, and something of what lies behind it."

"Please, I don't want to hear any more about the tapestry. I want to know about . . ." She paused. *There is nothing I want to know.* She wanted to cry, but instead the words dragged out of her: "The horse. I want to know about the horse."

"Ah, yes. Handsome, is he not? His name is Gabdon. He is an unusual creature. But you already know that, do you not?"

She nodded slowly.

"He came to you."

"No. That is yes. But only in a dream. I mean . . . Oh, I want the dreams to stop."

"They will not."

"But why? Why?" Jessica shouted.

Ashtar said nothing.

Then, as if someone had laid a heavy stone on her back, her shoulders drooped. "All right. What do I have to do?" she asked resignedly.

"You must remove the tapestry from the wall and roll it tightly. Then you must take it home with you and keep it safe." He stopped speaking.

She looked up in surprise. "That's all?"

He smiled. "For now, yes."

"Will someone come for it?"

"Someone may try. But you must give it to no one."

"From whom do I have to keep it safe? Or from what?" she asked. Then she said quickly, "Never mind. I don't want to know." And she walked over to the tapestry. "Gabdon," she murmured. Then, gently, she took it from the wall. Laying it on the ground, she began to roll it up.

"Tighter," Ashtar commanded.

She obeyed.

He produced a silken cord, and she tied it about the tapestry. When she was done, she held the bundle out to Ashtar. He bent and touched his forehead to it and then stood erect. She didn't understand the gesture, but asked nothing, only tucked the tapestry under her arm. "Now," she said, trembling slightly, "your word. You promised me that Jack is safe and that you would free him. Do it."

"As you command," Ashtar said. He faced the frozen figure. Then he raised his left hand and slowly opened and closed it three times. From it, a shaft of light, white and cold, struck the still figure.

Jessica heard a high-pitched scream, and then, senseless, she crumpled to the floor.

# 6

"YOU OKAY, now?"

*Have I been dreaming again,* she thought. *That funny little man with the turban. What was his name? Omar? Akbar? Ashtar? Yes, that was it—Ashtar. Brr. It was a dream, wasn't it? The dreams were bad enough, but they were better than—*

"Jess, are you okay?"

She looked up. Jack's tense white face drifted into focus.

"Have I been asleep?" she asked cautiously.

"No. Don't you remember? You fainted."

*No, I don't remember fainting,* she thought; but he looked so worried that she said, "I'm all right now."

She glanced around her. She was sitting propped against an ancient tree, near a watering trough, in front of a dilapidated building with a sign hanging tipsily from the roof.

"We stopped here," she said.

"Yes." He looked relieved.

*The little man, Ashtar had told some story—there was a shah in it or a vizier or something like that. And there was some sort of tapestry.*

"You really must still be weak from the flu. Rest a little longer, and then we'll head back."

*The flu, yes, maybe that was what did it. But it seemed so real. And that white light. A shaft of white light. And a scream. And Jack . . . Jack!*

"Jack!" she cried aloud. "Are you all right?"

"Me?" he said, confused. "Of course I am."

*Something is happening to me,* she thought. "Let's go back," she said, getting up quickly and running to the bike, still parked where they'd left it minutes, hours, days, ago.

"Sure. Hey, don't you want this antique?" He came toward her with a roll of dirty fabric in his arms.

She looked at it and gasped. "Gabdon!"

"What?" Jack said.

"Nothing," she answered rapidly. *Then it wasn't a dream. I'm going crazy. I must be,* she thought. *Even though Ashtar said . . . Oh no, I'm talking about him as if he were real.* "Oh no, no," she moaned.

Jack stopped tying the bundle of cloth to the back of the bike. "I better get you home. You really aren't well."

*You don't know just how sick I really am,* she thought and began to laugh.

"What's so funny?"

"Nothing . . . Everything," she said.

He looked at her for a minute and then went back to securing the tapestry. When he finished, Jessica asked as casually as she could, "Jack, do you believe in magic?"

"You mean spirits and stuff like that?"

"Well, sort of . . . but something higher . . . more powerful."

"Like God?"

"Yes and no. I'm not sure. A link maybe between times, worlds?"

"Na. Not really. I don't believe in God. I think there's only people. And not even them for very long. When we die, that's it."

"You mean you don't think people can have other lives?"

"Other lives? Jess, what are you talking about?"

"Never mind. Skip it."

"Okay." He shrugged and started the engine.

*Other lives. Reincarnation. How did I get started on that! I'm even starting to talk crazy,* she thought. *What am I going to do?*

She got on the bike. As they drove along, she tried to blot out the thoughts that pushed and shoved at her. *Calm down, calm down, and listen to the wind,* she told herself.

The wind sang in her ears. She was just beginning to relax when the windsong seemed to warp, and a silky voice, a voice that seemed to stir lazily from somewhere far away, whispered, *If you wish to fly on Gabdon, unroll the tapestry and call his name.*

Jessica turned her head from side to side. But there was no one about.

"Who are you?" she cried.

*A friend.*

"Where are you?"

*Near. Come, call the horse. You remember what it was like to soar on his back. He will take you away from all that is ugly and sad into a realm where all is peace and beauty.*

*Away from school? Away from my dingy house and my dreary town? Away from my mother?*

*Yes, yes,* answered the voice. *There is nothing to fear. Come. Come.*

*Ashtar said the tapestry had powers. And the horse . . . to fly on him. It was so beautiful.* "Jack," she called, "Jack!"

"What?"

"Stop the bike. STOP THE—" But she never finished the sentence, for suddenly some inexplicable rage tore through her. "No. No. You'll take him. You'll misuse him. You . . . you . . . beguiler." The strange word ripped from her throat.

"I can't understand what you're saying," Jack shouted, slowing the bike.

"Never mind. Just keep driving," she shouted back.

*Fool,* the silky voice spit at her. And then it was gone.

*Safe,* she thought, without knowing why.

But, as they turned down her street, the thought was hurled back at her. For there in the driveway of her house sat her mother's car.

# 7

WHEN I was born, the astrologer cast my chart. "She will be destined for great things," he said, "but . . ." He did not want to tell the rest, but my father bade him continue. "But not now," the puzzled astrologer answered. "What do you mean, fool?" my mother spat. "I do not know," he answered. My mother, in a fury, wanted him to be imprisoned until he found the answer, but my father prevented it. "Perhaps it is better not to know the future," he said, shocking everyone in the court. At least, this is the story the Magus told me.

I asked him what the story meant; he said in time I would discover the answer. But it has not yet revealed itself to me. And as I have already proven myself unable even to follow my father's dearest request, I begin to doubt the story's truth. For a time, I asked those about me what they thought it meant. My nursemaid laughed and then hid her mouth, the way she does. My handmaid Pati merely shrugged. And Gamesh looked disgusted and proclaimed it all a batch of nonsense anyway.

Gamesh. The memory of him pains deepest. He was my friend. When we were both too small to speak one another's name, we played together, sometimes in the courtyard, sometimes in the stable, clacking copper pots or stringing beads or chasing bright yellow-headed birds. We lost child teeth on the same day, splashed one another in the children's bath, suffered together from eating too many camhi nuts. But when I turned nine, my mother decided it was time for us to observe our proper stations. She tried to separate us. I blame her not—she was only acting as the queen she had been taught to be. And in any case, she did not succeed, although there grew more constraint between us as we each had to play our roles. Still, when it came time for me to learn to ride a horse, I screamed so for Gamesh that poor Pati had to go running for him. And when Gamesh hurt his leg and could not walk, I sat by his side every day, amusing him with impersonations of palace guards and servants. Finally, my mother gave up, or so I believed, and fixed her sight on a husband for me. I could hear her thinking, Soon you will have no time for your friend. Your heart must go to your husband.

She did not know that I intended—intend—to have no husband but Gamesh. My mother's spells, her incantations, her divinations, could not, will not, prise that secret from me; could never, will never, alter my choice. Even now, though he lies buried in the earth.

Oh Gamesh, I would weep for you, but they have taught me it is unseemly for a princess to weep. And even now, even here, in this No-Man's-Land, I am too well trained to disobey them.

# 8

"DAMN! The old battle axe is back! What the hell is she doing home so early?"

Jessica sat rigid on the seat of the motorcycle. Then, her brain finally grasping the situation, she jumped off the bike and shouted, "Get out of here, Jack!"

"I'm not leaving you alone to face her," he said, dismounting.

"It'll be worse if she finds out I've been with you. Now, go!"

He hesitated, but then climbed back on the bike. "I'll see you tonight," he said.

"No," she said.

"Yes." And he rode away.

Her mind whirling, Jessica walked the rest of the way to her house. *This is bad. I blew it this time*, she thought. *I'll lie. I'll tell her I took a walk. Mom can't have been home long, so she won't know the difference.* Nevertheless, Jessica was sweating, and her chest felt tight. *Relax*, she told herself. *Relax.*

When she reached the door, she fumbled for her key. Her palms were sweating again, and she had to wipe them on her jeans. The lock eluded her.

Suddenly, the door swung open, and she stumbled into the hall.

"Come in, Miss Hell's Angel," her mother said, slamming the door behind her.

Jessica wanted to whimper, but she stared coldly at her mother.

"The silent treatment, huh? I'll loosen your tongue." Her mother cuffed the side of her head.

Jessica recoiled, but quickly pulled herself erect. She was shivering and breathing hard, but she fought against tears. She hadn't wept since she was a little girl, and she would not weep now.

"Shameless! Just getting over the flu and you go riding through the streets proud as punch with that hoodlum!"

*Say nothing. Nothing.*

"Mrs. Schneider saw you. You nearly ran over her lawn, she said."

*Mrs. Schneider, the town busybody.*

"But that Jack is in for it now. Stealing a motorcycle! I hope they—"

"It wasn't stolen," she blurted out.

"Oh, it wasn't?" her mother said triumphantly. "I call taking someone's motorcycle without his knowledge stealing, even if that someone is your brother. That's the law."

Jessica said nothing, but her body trembled. Her mother often talked about "the law" as if legality were an inflexible entity encompassing the universe.

After a pause, her mother sighed and felt Jessica's forehead. "Go to your room."

Jessica's eyebrows shot up. That was all? No more sharp

words? No more slaps? She started up the stairs, still puzzled.

"You're probably having a relapse. You'll have to be home from school for another week."

"No!" she cried. "I'm fine."

Her mother sighed again. "Willful as ever. Listen, you'll do as I say. Go to bed and stay there."

School usually annoyed Jessica: the useless courses that never told her the why of things. But school was also a place she could go and be welcome, as it were, for eight hours. A place where she could escape from her dreams. She shuddered.

Then she forced herself to say calmly, "No, you can't do that."

"Do what? I'm not doing anything, nitwit. You've been out galavanting on a motorcycle when you've barely recovered from a bad case of influenza. You're going to need another two weeks in bed if you don't get up there now."

"I have a French test this Friday. Mr. Robichaud sent me a note."

Her mother let out an exasperated grunt. "I don't care about Mr. Robichaud. Get to bed!"

Filled with rage, Jessica walked stiffly and silently to her room.

She stretched out on her bed. Her head ached. *I hate her,* she thought. *I hate her, and she hates me. But it couldn't have always been that way. When I was little, when Dad was still here, she was different then. She laughed a lot and made me things: rag dolls and pajamas and little velvet dresses to wear on Christmas and New Year's Day. Her hands were soft and warm . . .*

*Forget it, Jessica. She might have loved you once, but not now. Now she hates you. Just like she hates Jack . . . Oh God, Jack! His parents must know by now. They threatened to send him to military school when he broke those windows. If he gets sent away . . . No, Jessica, don't think about it. Go to sleep. No, don't want to sleep. Don't want to dream. But I'm so tired . . .*

A distant whinny. Hazy, but there was the muzzle. The white star on the forehead. *Clop-clop.* The hooves on hard ground.

Her hand is outstretched. She calls, "Gabdon! Gabdon!"

She sat bolt upright in bed. "The tapestry!" she cried. "I've forgotten the tapestry!" But there was nothing she could do, not now. She collapsed on the bed in an agony of quiet she could not wholly understand. Then slowly her weariness took over and she slipped into sleep.

# 9

STONES AT the window. Jessica woke with a start. Jack at this hour, she wondered.

Another rattle at the window.

She rose silently and looked out on the broad lawn. A thin, dark shape flickered in and then out of sight.

She shook herself. *That lunatic*, she thought. Opening her door quietly, she peered into the gloom of the hall. No light under her mother's door. Good. Then, with the ease of years of practice, she slipped noiselessly down the stairs.

The kitchen window was open a crack. She bent down and, through it, whistled three short, rising notes. Then she waited.

Three short, descending notes answered from the yard.

Stifling a giggle, she eased the bolt on the back door and stepped into the chill air.

"Jack?"

"Here, Jess." His hand clasped her wrist and pulled her out of the moonlight. "Don't want us seen."

"You madman! What are you doing here tonight at this hour?"

He grinned in the darkness. "Told you I was coming."

"Your parents . . ." she began.

"Pulling that old stuff about military school again. Don't

worry. I'll get out of it. Got out tonight, didn't I? They thought I was safely locked in my room."

"Locked in your room?"

"Yeah, their latest trick. It's called Lock Up the Looney or Barricade the Bad Boy." He laughed.

"That's not funny."

"Sure it is. Anyway, they forgot about the window and the drainpipe. They always forget something. Listen, what about your old battle-axe?"

Jessica bit her lip. "I have to stay home from school another week. She says I'm having a relapse."

"I'd like to relapse her, the rotten—"

"Jack, stop! I do feel sick. And anyway, things are bad enough."

"She acts like it's your fault your father left her."

She flinched at the bald words. Then she snapped, "What would you like me to do? Run away from home?"

"Why not?"

"Very funny."

"I'm not laughing."

The air seemed to grow colder around them. Finally, Jack broke the silence.

"Almost forgot," he said. "Brought your antique."

Immediately her anger evaporated.

"The tapestry!" She felt her heart strike against her ribs.

"Yeah. Did a little job on it for you. Hope you like it."

"Wh-what? Did you open it up?" Her head felt dizzy, and she had to lean back against the rough wall of the house.

"Sure," he said, puzzled, "I had to open it to clean it."

"Cl-clean it?"

"Yeah, it was filthy. Hey, is something wrong?"

She didn't answer. Her stomach ached, and her legs felt unsteady.

"Here, let's look at it—in the moonlight."

"No," she said, and then caught herself. *You're going to make him suspicious* she thought. *Go ahead and look at it. Just be careful.* But she wasn't certain what she had to be careful about.

"All right," she finally said, "You open it."

Carefully, Jack unrolled the tapestry. The moon seemed to shift, throwing light directly on the form of the horse.

Jessica gasped. This wasn't, couldn't be the same tapestry. The one she had taken from the wall was dull brown and gray. But this one . . . Even by the pale light she could see that the horse sparkled brilliantly, covered with trappings of scarlet, azure, gold and silver. His mane and tail shone rich chestnut. And there, there on his forehead was a small, glowing white star. The star seemed to beckon her. "Know me, Know me," it said.

"Beautiful, isn't it?" Jack spoke. "There's something, well, lifelike about it."

A strange laugh broke from her. "Yes," she said, "there certainly is." She laughed again.

Suddenly, a light flicked on on the second floor of the house.

"Oh no, my mother's awake. Hurry," Jessica said, frantically rolling up the tapestry.

"Tomorrow. See you," Jack whispered, slipping into the night.

Jessica scurried inside, shivering and clutching the bundle behind her.

"Are you down there, Jessica?" her mother called foggily from the top of the stairs.

"Yes, mother. I woke up. I'm getting some milk."

"In the dark?"

"I just got down here." She sucked in her breath, praying the lie went unnoticed.

"Go back to bed as soon as you're finished. And stay away from the window. The air's chill tonight." The voice retreated, and presently she heard her mother's bedroom door close.

She sighed heavily. Then giggled. *The air sure is chill,* she thought.


THE TAPESTRY under her bed (she'd find a better place tomorrow), Jessica tried to settle down to sleep again. But her mind kept drifting over everything that had happened: the ride,

Ashtar and the tapestry, Jack and military school, her mother and her punishment. Then suddenly she wondered if Jack was right, if her mother did blame her because her father had left. It hurt to think about him—the tall, thin man with the tickly moustache who held her a lot and told her wonderful stories. She was only five when it happened. She remembered the morning. She had padded down the stairs to have pancakes. It was a Sunday. Her mother used to always fix pancakes on Sundays. They were her father's favorite breakfast. She was hungry, she remembered; she walked into the kitchen to get an orange, and there was her mother, leaning over the sink, not crying, not even making a sound, but her finger was bleeding, cut to the bone, dripping over a piece of stationery.

"What is it, Momma?" she asked.

"Nothing. I cut my finger," her mother answered.

"Does it hurt?"

And then her mother had begun to laugh. Not nice laughter. High-pitched laughter. Like the frightened whinny of a horse. Jessica got scared and tried to hold her mother's hand, but she was pushed away. Then her mother stopped laughing, washed and bandaged her finger and finished making the pancakes.

"Where's Daddy?" Jessica asked.

"Gone."

At first she thought her mother meant he was off on one of his frequent hunting trips—something that always disturbed Jessica, although she didn't exactly know why.

Then her mother repeated, "Gone. And not coming back." She clanged the plate on the table. "Eat your pancakes. You won't get any others."

That was all. Nothing more had ever been said for all the nine years since her father's leaving. And her mother had never made pancakes again since that morning.

*She couldn't blame me,* Jessica thought. *Couldn't. She's so mean. She must have driven him away. Not me. I loved him. But then why did he leave me? Why? I'll never forgive him for that. Never.* Jessica began to thrash on the bed, twisting in the blankets until a splatter of stones on the window made her start.

Another rattle.

Jack again?

She pushed off the tangled bedclothes and went to the window. Flickering among the bushes was a thin, dark shape.

Confused, she walked hurriedly downstairs, bumping into a banister and then berating herself.

At the kitchen window, she whistled as she had done before.

A pause. Then, the answering signal.

She slid back the bolt. "Jack, now what do you want?"

A heavy stillness.

"Jack, stop fooling."

A breeze stirred the black trees.

"Jack?"

The shape moved in and out of the trees, which began to blur, reform themselves. Hands appeared holding dull scimitars that flashed almost imperceptibly against the darkened sky. Heads emerged, crowned with helmets that held in place shaggy locks. Then, the army began to advance slowly upon her. She whimpered, stepped back and stumbled against something hard and smooth. She reached out a tremulous hand to it and drew up a dully gleaming skull. With a shriek, she thrust it away from her and spun wildly for her house.

It was gone. And in its stead, another great army, swords on high, advancing as slowly and precisely as the one now at her back.

With a cry, she dropped to the ground and felt beneath her palms, instead of grass, cool, gritty sand. "Oh God," she sobbed and tried to crawl away from the booted legs surrounding her. Then, something picked her up by the neck of her nightgown and flung her some feet from the men. She crouched, stunned and sore, on the sand, as a sword flashed down upon armor and left the dark air quivering with its ring. An amber light that was not the moon began to glow, illuminating the warriors, slashing and driving their curved blades.

She saw the pale sand grow red in patches. And the screaming faces of the men surging past her. And then the face of one young soldier as he shot by her, bleeding from the mouth and throat. It was Jack's face. Horrified, she flung her arms to the heaving air and cried, "Ashtar! Ashtar! Tell me what to do."

And out of the groaning babble of killing and dying voices came a silky one.

*Give us the tapestry*, it said. *Give us Gabdon or the battle will rage sweeping all in its path.*

She tottered to her feet, her eyes darting, fingers searching for the source of the voice.

*This is but a taste of what is to come. Give us Gabdon now, and you will be safe.*

Something was in her arms, soft and hard at once. She gazed at the cylindrical shape. No, it couldn't be. She had put it under the bed. In her room. In her house. But now the bed, the room, the house were gone. "How . . . how . . ." she stuttered.

*Give us Gabdon now*, commanded the voice. Then it began to chant, *Gabdon. Gabdon. Gabdon. Gabdon. Gabdon . . .* Each intonation beat in her ears like so many cracks of the horseman's whip. *Gabdon. Gabdon. Gabdon. Gabdon.*

"Stop it. Stop it!" Jessica shouted, writhing against the noise. "I'll give you Gabdon." She raised the tapestry above her head, poised to fling it into the roiling mass of bodies before her.

Suddenly, a white light. The suggestion of a fur-soft muzzle, the hint of eyes deep and sad, a star blazing above them. Beckoning. Pleading. And then a silence as deep as the eyes.

Jessica's arms lowered softly. She sensed a round, enclosing warmth never felt before. If she were to reach toward it . . . Something burgeoned far inside. She extended her arms and their burden to the star.

It sparked once and disappeared. Then, arms empty, Jessica was alone under a pale emerging moon on the grass behind her home.

*Mother, Mother.* She wanted to cry out the words, but they would not leave her lips. *Mother, Mother. What is happening to me? What is happening?* She sank to the ground and tore up handfuls of grass.

A light. Above the back door. "Jessica, are you out there?"

*Mother, Mother, keep away. I am cursed.*

"Jessica?"

"Here. Over here," she answered faintly.

"What the hell are you doing? Are you nuts? You really will get sick again."

Her mother pulled Jessica to her feet, brushed off the nightgown and peered into her face. "I don't know what's going on with you. Are you trying to make me crazy?"

"No. Tapestry. The battle . . ."

"You're really not well at all," her mother said, ashy in the moonlight.

"Where . . . where . . . where . . ."

"The flu again." She reached out to feel Jessica's forehead.

Jessica spun away. "No. No more killing!" she roared, and her face was white as the skull she had held in her hands.

Frightened, her mother retreated a step. "You're dreaming. Your father had vivid dreams. Sleepwalking dreams." She stopped, her face contorted with memory. Then she said softly, "Come. Come back to bed."

"No. Yes." Jessica shuddered and went limp. She let her mother propel her to the door.

Only then did she hear, faintly echoing, the low, silky, mocking laugh that pealed and then vanished into the cold night air.

# 10

WRITE THE correct English translation for the following phrases:

1) *J'ai faim.*

Jessica stared at the paper. Words, phrases. Black squiggles. Sitting in school taking silly French tests while the world was falling to pieces. Well, I'd rather be here than home. *Thanks for calling my mother, Mr. Robichaud. Have hardly slept for the past few nights. Afraid to sleep. Afraid to stay awake, too. Home isn't safe.* She looked down at the paper.

1) *J'ai faim.*

Laboriously she wrote down: 1) I am hungry. *But I'm not hungry. Je n'ai pas faim. Pas de tout.*

2) *Je suis triste.*

I am sad. *Yes, that was more appropriate. Three days. Not a word in three days. Not a sign since the night of the battle.* She shuddered. *It wasn't like him.* She'd tried calling his house, but hung up when his father answered. Now she looked up. Her neighbor Judy Callahan quickly turned her head away from Jessica's paper.

3) *Je suis sourd.*

I am deaf. *Or is it blind?* She hesitated, pen poised over her paper.

"But it's true," Judy Callahan whispered to Margie Schraeder.

"Really?"

"Yeah, military school for sure this time."

Jessica looked up sharply.

"Serves him right," Margie said.

She and Judy giggled and then looked at Jessica.

She felt herself flush with anger.

"Judy Callahan and Margie Schraeder, are you cheating?" Mr. Robichaud's voice boomed out.

"No, Mr. Robichaud," Judy said. "We were talking about Jack Manning."

The entire class giggled.

"Silence! This is an examination. You may talk about Jack Manning after school, not during it. Is that understood?"

"Yes, Mr. Robichaud," Judy replied. "We'll *certainly* talk about him *after* school."

The class laughed again.

"Silence!" Mr. Robichaud bellowed.

Jessica clenched her fists, pressing her nails into her palms. *I* want to punch them. *Punch them until they yell. Creeps! All of them! Jack will get out of it! He has to. He always does. Always!* Her eyes began to sting, but no tears came. She would not cry. She rubbed her eyes with a fist and looked down at her test.

4) *J'ai peur.*

I am afraid, she wrote slowly.


THE REST of the day was a torment. Titters and whispers in the halls, in the classrooms, in the cafeteria, in the gym. Did you hear about Jack Manning? He stole a bike. Manning was always bad. Did you hear about Jack Manning? Smashed up a bike. Drunk, probably. Did you hear about Jack Manning? Stole a car and they're sending him to reform school. Did you hear? Did you hear? Did you hear?

In history, Mr. Nadel gave the class a long lecture on the solid discipline of military schools and how good they are for boys like Jack Manning. Jessica asked to be excused. She fled to the toilet and was sick.

*Shut up, all of you; shut up,* she screamed inside. *Lies. Rumors. None of you cares. Not as long as you get to hear some good gossip. Maybe you're all lying about military school. Maybe he doesn't have to go.*

She sat down on the bathroom tiles and held her head in her hands until the bell rang.

After school, she raced to Jack's house. She didn't care if his father was home this time. But he wasn't. Jack's mother let her in. She was a thin, worn woman, who always looked frightened.

"It's all for the best," she said, half-heartedly.

"Is he in his room?" Jessica demanded.

"Yes, he won't come out."

Jessica tore upstairs and flung open his door. He was sitting on an old trunk in the corner of the room.

"Is it true?" she asked.

"Yep, it's true all right," he said grimly.

"But why?"

"Why not? I'm a hopeless case, according to my father. And

Mom's such a weakling she'd never open her trap to argue with him. Military school!"

"You can't go," she blurted out. He couldn't leave her to the soldiers. The soldiers and the voice. The mocking voice. She began to shake.

"Oh I'm going . . ." He lowered his voice. "But not to military school."

"What do you mean?"

"Tonight, I'm hitting the road."

"Wh-where are you going?"

"Well, my uncle's got a farm in Nebraska somewheres. He hates my dad's guts, so I'm sure he'd be happy to let me stay there."

"But Nebraska's a long way off. How are you going to get there?"

"The way any self-respecting runaway does—by hitching."

"Jack, you can't!"

He looked at her and said loudly, "Sure I can. So can you. How about coming along?"

She stared at him helplessly.

His eyes bored into hers. "I mean it," he said.

She shook her head and ran from the room.

AT HOME, she splashed cold water on her face and tottered to her room. She opened her closet door unwillingly. Yes, the thing was still there, high on a shelf behind a box of her baby clothes. She didn't want to think about it, but it was like that albatross she read about last year—the one that hung around the ancient mariner's neck—her burden to look after. How could such a beautiful thing be such a burden. She closed the door quickly and turned on the radio. Another war in the Middle East. Another animal on the verge of extinction. She felt sick again and shut off the set. *Must get out of here. Maybe I'd be okay somewhere else,* she thought. *Get my head together, as they say.*

But, exhausted, she threw herself on her bed. She had to rest. She couldn't go anywhere until she rested.

\* \* \*

The room begins to glow softly orange, red, yellow. Fire-light. Gently, a voice begins to hum a lullaby. Delicate perfume. Footsteps.

The lady comes smiling. She wears a fine red robe. Her black hair is hung in straight tight curls twined with gold. On her arms, neck are gold bangles. Heavy golden earrings set with dark blue stones hang from her ears. She holds out a golden cup filled with dark red liquid.

For me, Jessica asks.

The lady nods.

Jessica stretches out her hand.

But first, may I see the tapestry, the lady asks in a low, silky voice.

Jessica draws back her hand. The tapestry? What tapestry, she says.

The lady smiles. I think you know which tapestry.

Jessica says nothing.

Just a small look, the lady says. Do you not want the dreams to stop?

Jessica hesitates. You'll leave me alone, she asks.

Yes.

She stands up. Something soft as a mane brushes her cheek. She steps backwards. No, she says.

Come, come. Drink now, the lady says, and see if you will feel more generous.

No, Jessica shouts, knocking over the cup. No!

Fool, says the lady, and laughs. The mocking laugh that Jessica has heard before.

No, Jessica shouts again. "No!"

"NINCOMPOOP. Stop shouting."

She opened her eyes.

Her mother, looking upset, was standing where the lady had been.

"She's gone," Jessica said, panting.

"You've been dreaming again," her mother said.

"Did you see her?"

Her mother stared at her. "Are you getting sick again?" She stretched out a hand.

Jessica pulled away. "I'm fine," she said quickly.

Her mother stiffened and dropped her hand. "Good. How was the French test?"

"The French test? It was okay," she said, distractedly.

"Fine. I thought you might like to go out to dinner tonight."

Jessica exhaled deeply. Then she looked at her mother. "What did you say?"

Her mother repeated the invitation. "To Frenchy's. Ha-ha, Frenchy's after a French test. That's funny."

She hesitated, tempted. Frenchy's had good food. And she didn't want to be in this house. "Well . . ."

"You can have shrimp scampi."

"Okay."

"Good." Her mother smiled. "We'll toast to Jack's new scholastic career."

She went cold. There was no way to refuse now. Her mother had won again. "I think I'd like to nap some more," she said, tight-lipped.

"Good idea." At the doorway, her mother paused. "Maybe at last you'll make some nice friends," she said, and closed the door.

Jessica picked up her pillow and threw it hard at the door. Her face felt strained, as if the skin around her eyes were stretched to breaking. Suddenly she rose and walked to the mirror. Staring at herself, she breathed deeply and then muttered, "You haven't won, Mother. I'm going with Jack. Did you hear that? I'm going with Jack!"

*TEN PAST midnight. Isn't she ever going to bed? Maybe she's fallen asleep in front of the TV the way she sometimes does,* Jessica wondered. *Or maybe she's guessed and is waiting —like the cat at the mouse's hole.*

*Quarter past midnight. Oh God, what if he's already gone? I'd never find him. Never. And I'd be left here to go crazy.*

Then she heard the television click off and the familiar footsteps drag wearily upstairs. When her mother's door closed, she quickly pulled her knapsack from under the bed. Underwear, socks, toothbrush and paste, spare jeans, shirt, sweater, hairbrush, favorite book of fairy tales she had never grown too old for. She had packed with great care hours before. Now she removed her nightgown and tucked it into the sack. Already fully dressed, she grabbed the knapsack and scurried from the room. She was halfway down the stairs when she remembered the tapestry.

She didn't want to take it. *Maybe they'll leave me alone*, she thought, *if I don't have it. Whoever they are.* Then she thought, *No, take it. Nobody is after you. And if they are, then at least you'll know you're not nuts. And besides, Jack will be there.* She turned back upstairs.

She lifted the box down carefully. The tapestry was there, waiting, warm and rough. Even rolled up, it seemed to shine in the faint light, little sparks glinting here and there. She gently lifted it down. It seemed heavier. It was going to weigh her down, but she gathered it and the knapsack and hurried downstairs and into the street.

She had gone only a few paces when an apparition arose before her.

"Mother," she stammered.

"No, dummy. I'm not your mother."

"Jack! I was coming to—"

"I know," he said softly. "I knew you would."

"How?"

And then he kissed her.

Startled and confused, she pulled back. What was happening? Jack was her friend, her brother in rebellion. Wasn't that how he thought of her?

"I'm sorry," he said stiffly, averting his face.

"No, it's all right. It's just . . . you never . . ."

"Don't." He paused, then asked, "What are you carrying?"

She knew he was still hurt, but she couldn't think of anything else that would smooth over what had happened, so she replied, "Knapsack."

He nodded.

"And the tapestry," she added reluctantly.

But he merely nodded again and said, "Okay, let's go."

She turned briefly and looked at her house. Her mother would have to take care of it all by herself now, she thought, with a twinge of remorse.

"She'll survive," Jack said, reading her mind.

"Let's go," she said.

They walked quickly through the empty streets. The houses seemed like sleeping strangers. Soon they were out on the same road they'd ridden on the motorcycle.

Blackness. Blackness everywhere. She felt it pressing in on her. She stopped walking and looked up at the sky. Moon and stars and blackness. *If I lie on the ground and look up, it might look pretty*, she thought, *pretty and not so vast.*

"Come on, Jess," Jack called. "Here comes a car."

They stuck out their thumbs expectantly. The car sped by.

"Well, better luck next time," he said, and they walked on.

*AN HOUR. We've been walking an hour*, she thought. *Two cars have gone by and neither stopped. I'm going to pass out if we don't get a lift soon.* She pulled the collar of her jacket higher and leaned against a telephone pole.

"Here, have some candy." Jack pushed half a chocolate bar toward her.

She took it gratefully. "What do you think your parents will do?" she asked.

"Call the cops. They're not very original."

"The police!" She winced. Somehow, she hadn't thought about the police looking for Jack—and for her.

"Don't worry, we'll be long gone before my parents even get up, let alone sic the cops on us."

He was interrupted by the distant sound of an approaching car. It was still about half a mile away, but even from where they were they could see the searchlights sweeping the roadside.

"Oh no," Jessica shouted. "Hide. We have to hide."

"Where?" he rapped out.

She looked around. The road was flat, empty. Dark, treeless fields stretched out on either side.

"No, there's no place," he answered. "Drop down and lie flat. Maybe they won't see us."

The car was very near. It would pass them any second now. Her face in the wet grass, she prayed, "Please don't, please, please. Her hand reached out and touched the tapestry.

Suddenly, a bolt of white light shot from it. She cried out and pulled back her hand as the car rumbled by.

"What the hell was that? Lightning?" Jack yelled.

"I . . . I . . ." She couldn't answer. She squeezed her hand—it was trembling, but there was no pain. Then she said, "You saw it too?"

But he just said, "Keep watching the road."

She looked up. The police car had stopped. She found her voice. "Jack, no, they're turning back!"

"Damn, they've seen us!"

Blindly, they broke into a run.

Behind them, the police horn boomed out, "Stop immediately. This is the police."

The car began to move.

"Faster. Into the field."

They ran into the wheat stubble. The car gathered speed.

"Run, Jess, run."

Closer. She felt the searchlights begin to burn into the back of her skull.

*My God, we'll be killed,* she thought.

And then Jack stumbled.

"No!" she screamed.

"My ankle!" he howled. "Jess, leave me and keep running!"

But Jessica was frozen, watching the car hurtling toward them.

"NOW!" a voice commanded. "It is time."

She recognized the voice. It was Ashtar.

Instantly, she knew what to do. Ripping the thin cord holding it, she unrolled the tapestry.

"NOW!" Ashtar's voice ordered.

"GABDON!" she shrieked.

And the night grew white, brilliant. The ground shook with hoofbeats. And, resplendent in red, azure, gold and silver trappings, a chestnut horse with a glowing white star on his forehead reared up before her. He gazed at Jessica with large gleaming, implacable eyes.

"Lord!" Jack shouted, his eyes wide with terror.

"Ahhh," Jessica gasped. "You're real. Oh God, you *are* real."

But she had no time to think of the implications. Quickly, she hoisted Jack up onto the saddle and climbed up in front of him. "Hold onto me," she commanded, and then, "Yaru, yaru, Gabdon!"

The horse thundered off as the car bore down on them.

"Yaru, yaru," Jessica yelled.

The horse's powerful muscles pulled faster. His hooves rang on tarmac now.

But the police car was gaining on them.

"Yaru," she shouted, and then, "Aly-mai."

The hooves clattered on the road and then were silent.

The road, fields, police car shrank beneath them. The moon, stars spun dizzyingly nearer. An owl flew, shrieking, from their path. And Jessica threw her head back, looked at the sky and laughed.

# 11

THE MAGUS spoke the truth. There are undreamed of wonders in this world. What I have seen . . . oh, what have I seen?

"Look," the Magus said. "Look." The veil parted, and I saw,

in a small circle as if I were standing on Kadi's Hill looking through a glass at the valley below, the horse. The horse from the tapestry. And a girl who could master him. She was so strong, so certain. And though she was far from me, I saw the ma-lat shining in her. She called the horse, and he came. She can, she will do what I could not. She will protect the horse; she will keep him safe; she will, somehow, bring him to my father so that once more he will take his rightful position, unite our kingdom in peace and harmony and heal the hearts of our people.

Although I cried out to the Magus to let me gaze longer, the vision departed as quickly as it came. But even as the veil closed once more, the Magus' voice, clear and full of light, came to me. "You will see her again. And you will know her."

# 12

SHE GAZED at the sky. Gabdon was gone. The tapestry lay in her arms, neatly rolled and tied once more. She had spoken, and the horse had vanished; but she could not remember the words. *I fought this*, she thought, *I fought it, but it's happening anyway*.

"I hurt, Jess," Jack moaned.

He was lying on the ground at her feet. She shook herself the way a dog does after a bath. "Oh Jack, I'm sorry. Here, lean on me." She helped him into the cold parlor. Once inside, he passed out.

"How pleasant to see you again," said the dry voice.

"Ashtar!" Jessica exclaimed.

He smiled and bowed.

"Ashtar, why are we here? What's going on? Who is the lady? Who are . . . ?"

"Let us first tend to your friend," he interrupted, inclining his head toward Jack, who lay pale and silent. "Then perhaps I will answer some of your questions."

"Will he be all right?" she asked anxiously as Ashtar stooped to examine Jack.

Ashtar said nothing, but removed a length of cloth from his robe and deftly went to work. When he finished, he stood up and said simply, "His ankle is fractured. I have set it, but he must lie quietly for many days to come."

"Oh no," Jessica sighed heavily and sat beside Jack.

His eyelids fluttered open, and he looked at her, at first un-comprehendingly and then with fear. "Where are we?" he said hoarsely.

"Hello and welcome back," she said ruefully. "We're in the old farmhouse. The one where we found the tapestry."

"How did we get here?"

"Don't you remember?"

"I remember something, but it couldn't have . . . it must have been a dream."

Then Jack saw Ashtar, and he cried out and tried to raise himself from the floor.

"No, don't. You've broken your ankle," Jessica said gently. "But you're safe—we're safe."

He sank back on the mat and rasped at Ashtar, "Who the devil are you?"

Jessica, too, looked at Ashtar, her eyes demanding an answer.

"A good question," Ashtar replied. "Let us say for now that I am an historian. Also, I am skilled at mending fractured ankles."

"And at sliding out of answers," Jack said. Then he glanced at the thick bandage around his foot. "You did this?"

Ashtar bowed again. "It will heal, but you must not walk on it for some time."

"Not walk on it! What am I supposed to do? Lie here and die. Or let the police find me and drag me back to my parents and military school," he said bitterly.

"I believe there is another alternative," Ashtar answered.

Jessica had not taken her eyes off Ashtar.

"Yes, I can take care of him," she said.

"Correct," said Ashtar. "And necessary."

"Necessary? Why necessary?" Jack demanded. "I can't move, can't do anything. It's not safe for her here with an invalid who can't help look for food or run from the cops. It's not safe."

"On the contrary, Master Jack, this is the only place where it is safe."

Jessica and Jack both began to speak, but Ashtar silenced them and began his story.

"Once, many centuries ago, there was a land where powerful gods looked down and wondered how to end the strife of a people who worshipped them. Meltar, God of the Sun and the Grain, Bodar, Goddess of the Moon and the Rivers, Golgon, God of the Underworld, Tecti, Goddess of Healing, Jamala, Goddess of Transformation, Padish, God of Enlightenment—and all the other gods—assembled in their great hall. They had a long debate. Some favored destroying the people, and some favored abandoning them. But some wished to teach them peace.

" 'We have tried to do that in the past,' said Golgon, 'and they have failed to learn.'

" 'We must try once more,' argued Bodar.

"And so it was decided.

" 'Who among us shall try to teach them?' asked Meltar. 'Whom shall we choose?'

" 'I shall do it,' spoke Tecti. 'I am a healer.'

" 'I shall do it. I bring revelations,' said Padish.

" 'I shall do it,' said Jamala. 'I cause change.'

"But it was Kadi, the Horse God, God of Swiftness and Essence, who was chosen.

" 'What shall you do, Brother?' Bodar asked him.

" 'I shall send my son to the people, and I shall appoint one to master him. One in whom the ma-lat shines bright. And for as long as the Horsemaster keeps my son safe and uses him for the good of the people, so shall peace that long reign.'

" 'Whom shall you choose?'

" 'I know not,' answered Kadi. 'But I shall know when he is born.'

" 'And what will happen when that Horsemaster is no more? Will you choose another?' asked Bodar.

" 'No. I will not,' said Kadi. 'The next Horsemaster will become so through his own strength and through the support of his people.'

" 'But suppose a strong, evil person should arise and gain the people's allegiance? Would you allow that person to become Horsemaster,' asked Meltar.

"Kadi let out a long sigh. 'I would allow it. If the people do not learn wisdom from a Horsemaster chosen by the gods themselves, there is nothing further we can do to teach them.'

" 'What if there is more than one contender for Horsemaster? What if there is a struggle?'

" 'Then so be it.'

" 'Harsh,' said Bodar.

" 'But just,' said Meltar.

"Then the voice of Golgon, God of the Underworld, said, 'What if the Horsemaster *you* choose fails? What if the people turn from him? What if such a one appears who is stronger than your Horsemaster and perhaps even you yourself, Kadi?'

But the gods scoffed at Golgon. Such a thing could never happen, they said.

"Many years passed and there sprang up the legend that one day a Horsemaster would come to rule the land in peace. Many kings were born and died and finally there came a great one named Azan. He had two sons, Cambyses the younger and Tarkesh the elder. Tarkesh was the king's favorite—a boy with such gentleness the shy gazelles would graze at his feet and with such wisdom the clever ravens would listen with awe when he spoke. For this, Cambyses despised him and swore vengeance. But because he was a mere boy his words were disregarded.

"Now, at Tarkesh's birth, the great god felt a tremor in his heart. He looked down upon the child and smiled for he saw in him a great spirit. On the boy's twelfth birthday, he came to King Azan in a dream. 'Your son shall be my avatar on earth. And he shall reign wisely and well. You shall say nothing to him. But on his thirteenth birthday, you shall give him my gift, which you will find in the royal stables.'

"King Azan awoke, trembling and pale. 'My son. Horse-master!' he whispered. But he held his tongue. And on Tarkesh's thirteenth birthday, he honored his son with a great feast and Kadi's gift—a marvelous horse, which wore a tapestry of itself over its back. Great was Tarkesh's pleasure and Cambyses's fury. Again he swore vengeance. And again he was ignored."

Here, Ashtar paused significantly, but Jack impatiently demanded, "Well, what *did* happen?"

"Have no fear, Master Jack," Ashtar said. "I will tell you. One month after his thirteenth birthday, Tarkesh disappeared. The king searched the kingdom, but to no avail. When one of his servants suggested that Cambyses be questioned, he was soundly beaten. The king and all his subjects mourned for Tarkesh—all but Cambyses and his followers.

"When the king himself died, it was Cambyses who succeeded him. Cambyses ruled badly. He was often drunk and was known for his evil temper. And then, one day, a herald appeared from the North announcing the coming of Tarkesh, the kingdom's rightful ruler. Cambyses, the herald told all present, had planned to have Tarkesh slain; but the plan was discovered and Tarkesh was secreted to a fortress far away from the palace where he grew to be a man, as wise and as gentle as he was a boy.

"Cambyses railed at the herald, called him a liar and sent him in disgrace from the palace; but there were many who believed the herald and soon the followers of Tarkesh grew in number. Cambyses's own followers urged him to summon the man who called himself Tarkesh. Greet him graciously, they said, and then expose him as an imposter. To this Cambyses agreed.

"So, Tarkesh, his wife, his daughter and his son were sent for. A great feast was commanded, and thousands were invited to attend. The banquet hall was a mile long, hung with flowing purple and gold hangings and set with tables bearing delicacies from all corners of the kingdom. When Tarkesh appeared, Cambyses embraced him and enjoined him to partake freely of the sweetmeats, the wine, the entertainment.

"On the first day of the feast, Cambyses proposed a toast to the new king. 'But first,' he said, 'a toast to our tutor who has passed to his reward this year. Tarkesh, my brother, praise him.'

"Tarkesh stood up and spoke humbly, 'A toast to Zedon, who taught me the goodness of learning.'

"Cambyses's smile twisted, for Tarkesh had called the tutor by the correct name, but he said, 'A fine tribute, my brother.'

"On the second day of the feast, Cambyses again proposed a toast—this time to their father's fifth wife, who had been kind to the brothers when they were children. 'But you praise her, my brother; your words are finer than mine,' said Cambyses.

"Again Tarkesh stood and spoke, 'Much praise to Hadar, whose beauty was of face and of soul.'

"Cambyses's brows blackened, for again Tarkesh had spoken the proper name; but again he said, 'A fine tribute, my brother.'

"On the third day of the feast, Cambyses talked and joked loudly with his guests. He ordered dancers and musicians to perform and then called for a fortune-teller who sprinkled sand into mounds on a golden table.

" 'Seer, what do you see in my brother's future?' Cambyses asked.

"The fortune-teller looked at the sand and said, 'A kingdom, but then a great loss.'

"Cambyses smiled, thinking the loss was not far off. 'And for me?' he said.

"Again the fortune-teller sprinkled sand and looked at the mounds it made. Then he shuddered and fell to his knees.

" 'What do you see?' demanded Cambyses.

" 'Oh my lord,' said the fortune-teller. 'Do not command me to tell you.'

" 'I do command you,' roared Cambyses.

" 'Then my lord, I will tell you. I see Death.'

"Cambyses stumbled to his feet. 'Take him away. Away!' he

bellowed. Then he whirled around to face Tarkesh. 'Well, my brother,' he said with a sneer. 'A toast to your horse that our father gave you on your thirteenth birthday.'

"Tarkesh stood. He faced his brother, and then said quietly, 'Praise to Gabdon, the finest stallion I have owned. And here, Cambyses, is the very tapestry that was made of him.'

"When he unrolled the tapestry, Cambyses shrieked and grabbed his brother by the throat.

"The guards seized Cambyses and imprisoned him in his rooms where he was found the next morning, his throat slit and the golden knife that did the deed clutched in this hand.

"And so Tarkesh became king and Horsemaster."

Here Ashtar paused.

"Gabdon," Jessica whispered. "Gabdon."

"Yes, my child, Gabdon. The Horse God's own son."

# 13

HEAT. HIGH heat. Hot sand under her feet. Feet in sandals. Golden sandals. Golden sandals. Purple robe.

Sitting pressed. On the hill. Crowds around below. Herself set apart. But pressed between. She turns. Next to her, the Red Lady, smiling, pointing. Pointing to something below in the valley. Water. Lake. She wants to throw off sandals, robe, run naked to the lake, stop being pressed.

Procession winding slowly down to the lake. Far below. Someone naked being led down, down by priests.

She rises to her feet, horror growing inside.

The procession marches. The Red Lady smiles and points, smiles and points.

The naked boy is in the water. A priest lays a hand on his head. The boy kneels, opens his mouth and screams her name. Screams. His voice is Jack's. The priest pushes his head beneath the water.

"NO," SHE GASPED, biting her tongue. The lake, hill, boy, all gone. Jack, his arm flung across her shoulders, stirred beside her. Still breathing heavily from the horror of the dream, she sat up and looked around. The police, the farmhouse, Gabdon. It all came back to her. She leaped to her feet and ran out the door.

"Ashtar?" she called, her mouth dry, "Ashtar?"

He appeared behind her, carrying a warm bowl and a cup.

"Come inside and break your fast."

"Ashtar, I dreamed . . . " she began.

"I know."

"Someone in the water."

"Yes."

"Drowning . . ."

"Come inside, Jessica," he said gently.

She stopped, bewildered, and followed him inside.

Groggily, Jack sat up. He looked around. "So, it's true," he finally said.

Jessica sat down beside him and patted his hand.

Ashtar handed her the bowl and fetched another for Jack.

Jack stirred the cooked grain. "Is this manna?" he asked drily.

"It is rather more like your oatmeal," Ashtar replied.

They ate silently. Then Jack said, "We didn't hear the rest of your fairy tale."

"Fairy tale?"

"That cock and bull story you were telling us last night before you cast some sleep spell and knocked us out."

"I will tell you the rest," Ashtar replied calmly, "but first finish your meal."

"First you must sleep, first you must eat," Jack burst out. "Who do you think you are, ordering us around like little children?"

Ashtar turned to him and said in a stern voice, "The story I tell is one of great passion, of great sorrow. To bear it, you must be strong. Strong of body and strong of spirit."

"My body isn't exactly strong right now." Jack scowled, glancing at his ankle.

"That will mend. It is your stubborn spirit that concerns me. But then, you have always been stubborn."

"What the hell are you talking about?"

But Ashtar gazed into Jack's eyes, and Jack said no more.

"Now," Ashtar said, "I believe it is time to continue the story."

"With the tapestry of Gabdon hanging proudly in his royal chamber, Tarkesh set to work to unite the kingdom and to teach the people peace. One by one, the people opened their hearts to the wise shadoor. He did not call himself Horsemaster, but his legend reached all the corners of the land. For many years, peace reigned there. And some people began to wonder if the legend had finally come true. But Talliya, the wife of Tarkesh and a woman of great beauty, grew steadily discontent. The harmony between them disappeared. There were other lands—lands to the south, to the east—which were not ruled by Tarkesh. The people there did not open their hearts to him, nor were they likely to without force, thought Talliya.

" 'You are a king,' she said to her husband. 'You have power. Much power. Why do you not use this power?'

"And Tarkesh replied, 'What power would you have me use?'

"Talliya curved her full red lips and said in a voice low and silky, 'The power to conquer.'

"Then Tarkesh said harshly, 'There has been enough conquest. I use my power to raise souls, not to bend them.'

"Talliya answered, 'You must bend them to raise them.'

" 'Enough, my queen,' Tarkesh commanded. 'Enough.'

"And Talliya bowed and smiled. 'I bend to your wishes, my lord,' she said.

"That night, Talliya felt Tarkesh leave their bed. She followed him at a discreet distance. He walked slowly into the royal chamber and stood before the tapestry.

" 'Oh Gabdon, I beg your help. I am uneasy,' he said. 'I adore Talliya and desire only her happiness. But I cannot grant her wishes. I am Horsemaster in this land. I have taught my people peace. Yet I cannot teach my wife to still her restless heart . . .' The rustle of Talliya's robe made him pause, but he could not see her in the dim light. 'I must retreat, my friend. I shall go North. There I may gather strength to pass through this troubled time. I cannot take you with me. I must go alone— only then can I know myself.'

"Neither Gabdon nor Kadi answered him. Talliya left him standing there with a bowed head and slipped back into the bed-chamber.

"Within a fortnight, Tarkesh left for the North. He asked his daughter to guard the tapestry, but he did not tell her, just as he had not told Talliya, what power it held. After Tarkesh left, Talliya summoned the most eminent maguses of the court. Talliya had sometime before begun to practice magic, but she had not yet thrown in her lot with those who use it to bend.

" 'I wish to know a thing,' she told the magicians. 'A small thing.'

" 'Be it great or small, your majesty, only name it and it shall be known,' they said.

" 'I wish to know who wove the tapestry that hangs in the royal chamber and if he still lives.'

"The maguses laughed. 'Done,' they said, thinking that the thing was but a trivial matter.

"But it was not. First, they searched the stone tablets. No-where was the name to be found. Next, they asked discreetly about the court, but no one could answer. Finally, they turned to magic. But their sands and crystals, their entrails and incan-tations would not yield up the name.

"Finally, they gathered in the temple. 'He must be a power-ful magus. One who does not wish his name known,' one ma-gician said.

" 'Then he still lives,' said another.

" 'Yes.'

" 'And hides.'

" 'Yes.'

" 'Then, there is but one way to find him,' said the eldest magus.

" 'One way?'

" 'One way. The Law of Al-tonah.'

" 'The Law of Al-tonah! But he has committed no treason.'

" 'He will. Bid him to come for the service of our Lady Talliya.'

"A fire was lit in the temple. The maguses gathered around it. 'Come, O Magus of the Tapestry. Come for the service of Talliya, Lady of the land. Come as you are bound,' they chanted.

"Silence. No one came.

" 'He has broken the law. All magicians pledge to serve the king and queen as well as higher masters. So it was decreed by our forebear Al-tonah in the uprising of Malabek. Now he must appear by decree or he shall have his magic stripped from him. Send the order!' the eldest magician said.

"The order was sent.

"The maguses waited.

"A day passed. Two days.

"On the third, the magician appeared. He was a small man, brown and wizened, not at all what the others expected. Save for his eyes, which bespoke of a power great enough to frighten even those in the temple.

" 'You have commanded me by the Law of Al-tonah, and I have obeyed.' His voice was dry and angry as the sands.

" 'We have so commanded,' said the eldest magician. 'Why did you force us to invoke the law?'

" 'That you cannot compel me to answer. Now that you have summoned me, what do you desire?'

" 'We desire nothing. But perhaps the Lady Talliya does. We will advise that you attend her.'

"The hall was long and cold. Talliya sat at the end on a golden throne, a throne that tried to imitate the sun, but failed. The magician entered and approached warily.

" 'There is no need to tread so lightly, Magus,' Talliya said, and smiled. She turned to her servants. 'All of you, go,' she commanded.

"The magician waited.

"When the servants were gone, Talliya smiled again and asked, 'Your name, Magus?'

" 'You do not need my name, Lady. It was not for that you asked that I be found.'

" 'True. You are wise.' She motioned to him to sit.

" 'I will stand.'

" 'As you wish. Was your journey a difficult one?'

" 'You did not summon me to ask about my journey.'

" 'Again true. I believe you know what it is I wish.'

" 'You wish to know the secret of the tapestry.'

" 'You are wise indeed, Magus.'

" 'You do not need me for the answer, Lady. Your shadoor knows.'

" 'He does not care to tell me.'

" 'Then he has good reason.'

"Her eyes narrowed. 'I will know, Magus,' she hissed. Then, in a silkier voice, 'For my husband's sake.'

"The magician was silent.

" 'I believe the tapestry has some power to make him great,' she continued.

" 'He is now great,' the magician said sternly.

" 'He can be greater still. Now, Magus, I want to know what is that power.'

"The magician said nothing.

" 'We are both fond of magic, Magus. By that bond, tell me.'

"The Magus's eyes grew hard. 'The magic in which you dabble and which you seek to control is not the same as the Magic I hold true.'

"Talliya rose and spat, 'By the Law of Al-tonah, you will tell me.'

"The magician looked beyond Talliya. He raised his hand as though to stop something. Then a great tiredness came over him and his head drooped.

" 'The secret of the tapestry is the power of Gabdon. And the power of Gabdon is immense,' he said quietly.

"Talliya's eyes glittered in the light of the golden throne. 'How immense?' she demanded.

" 'The rider is Horsemaster.'

" 'So, it is true. I thought it was merely a legend the people made up to explain their obedience to my husband.'

" 'It is true—or so it was.'

" 'Was?'

" 'If Tarkesh does not come back for Gabdon—or receive him willingly, then . . .'

" 'Then?'

" 'Then he is nothing—and a new Horsemaster will arise.'

" 'A new Horsemaster,' Talliya whispered. Then she flung herself against her throne, threw back her head and laughed. 'A new Horsemaster,' she roared.

"The magician stared into the gold of the throne and murmured, 'Thus it spins.'

"That night a candle flickered in the royal chambers, its light falling on the tapestry of Gabdon. And Talliya, holding the taper, whispered, 'Great Horse, why should it be Tarkesh who is Horsemaster? He is so weak, a gazelle more than a man. He is ready to give up the power. There are those who are stronger . . .' A sound behind her made her pause. She turned.

"It was her daughter, trembling in the doorway.

" 'What is it, Noura,' Talliya snapped.

" 'I saw . . . I saw . . .' Noura panted.

" 'What did you see?'

" 'Blood. And water . . .'

" 'What else?' Talliya asked, frightened.

" 'My friend Gamesh . . . hurt. And then, a battle.'

"Talliya smiled with relief. She had little use for Gamesh. 'Go back to bed. It was only a dream.'

"Noura bowed and left the room.

"A battle, Talliya thought, and smiled.

"Quickly she set to work. A word here. A coin there. A caress. All bought enemies for Tarkesh. Tarkesh was unfaithful. Tarkesh was cruel. Tarkesh was a coward. Look how his wife wept at his name. Tarkesh favored the people of the North. Tarkesh was stirring the Northerners to arise, to form a separate kingdom. But his son, Smerdis, his son was pure, wise and brave. A perfect prince—a perfect shadoor—a perfect Horsemaster. Smerdis himself, hearing the talk, preened and grew fat. And in the palace, the people whispered.

"Some say word reached Tarkesh far in the North, visiting those who had once kept him safe. And that Kadi himself spoke to his Horsemaster and urged him to go home, to help his wife ease her desire for power, to teach peace to her and their son. But Tarkesh did not return.

"In the heavens, Kadi grew angry. Golgon's questions resounded in him: What if the Horsemaster *you* choose fails? What if someone appears stronger than your Horsemaster and perhaps even than you yourself, Kadi? In his anger, the Horse God turned his face from the people.

"It was then that Talliya made her choice. One night, in secret, she donned a red robe and crept silently into a little room for which only she held the key. There, she drew a circle, and there she walked 'round and 'round against the earth's wheel. What demons she stirred up, I know not—or even if she stirred any at all—save the demon in herself. But the ma-lat, twisted and dark, filled her. And she was no longer Talliya, but the Red Lady who called for blood.

"Talliya's daughter, Noura, sensed the change and grew frightened. Everyday she went to see that the tapestry was in place, and it always was. She did not know what more to do, so she went to her friend, the blacksmith's son, who was stoking the fire at the forge.

" 'Gamesh,' she said, 'there has been strange talk, evil talk against my father. What do you know of this?'

"Gamesh raised his head, his face dark with the heat. He had heard much. 'Since you ask, I will tell you. But you must not strike me.'

" 'Tell me.'

" 'It is said your mother has told tales of your father's cruelty and more.'

" 'You lie.'

" 'I do not lie,' he said quietly.

" 'Why should she tell such lies? My father is never cruel.'

" 'It is said she wants his throne for Smerdis—and herself.'

" 'Enough. I do not believe you,' she said coldly and walked to the garden.

"She sat under a pomegranate tree, and had been sitting there nearly an hour when the Magus appeared. She looked up, startled.

" 'Who are you?' she asked.

" 'I am a friend. What Gamesh tells you is the truth.'

"She stared at him.

" 'How do you know what Gamesh told me?' she asked.

" 'I know much about you.' He sat by her side and told her things about herself. She gazed at him in wonder. Then she shook her head. 'No, I do not believe you.' Angrily, she rose to her feet.

"He laid a hand on her arm and said quietly, 'Know you of the Horsemaster?'

"His words puzzled her. Finally, she replied, 'It is a story I heard when I was a child. The Horsemaster, chosen by Kadi, brings peace. But he needs the Horse God's son to rule. And the Horse God's son must be . . .' She groped for the phrase.

'Held in time out of time.'

'Yes, that is it. I never understood what that meant.'

'Noura, the Horse God's son is here. In time out of time,' the Magus said.

She stared at him.

" 'He is Gabdon, who hangs so proudly in your father's royal chamber.'

"Her small hand flew to her mouth. 'No, I do not believe you. My father . . . Horsemaster . . . I have heard tales . . . but, Horsemaster? My father!'

" 'Your father is in grave danger. Your mother knows the secret of his power.'

"She paled. But then her mouth hardened, and she taunted, 'But how, Magus, if he is Horsemaster, can she hurt him?'

" 'He has retreated to escape your mother's influence; and Kadi in his wrath has turned his face from him, and from the people. Now whosoever knows the secret and has the strength can seize the tapestry and use it for good—or for ill. Your mother knows the secret. And she has the strength. Unless your father returns—or unless Gabdon is brought to him and he accepts him once more—your mother, with her son, will usurp him.'

" 'You lie like the others, Magus,' Noura said sharply. 'Like Gamesh, another false friend. My mother and brother would not—' But she stopped abruptly, for the Magus had laid a finger to his lips and then pointed to the center of the courtyard. She followed his gesture. Two men were approaching, the keeper of the horse and Gamesh's father, the heavy-jowled blacksmith. They stood near the tree, but they did not see Noura and the Magus.

" 'We will take him when he returns.'

" 'Not without battle. He still has followers.'

" 'But Smerdis has more.'

"They laughed and walked on.

"Noura sat quite still. And when she turned her head, the Magus was gone. Then she rose and ran to the forge. Gamesh was hammering a sword blade. Sparks shot from the steel, surrounding Gamesh's head and arms in a wreath of gold.

" 'Gamesh, it is true.'

"He did not look at her, but struck harder at the metal.

" 'And your father is one of them.'

"With a cry, he flung down the blade. 'My father!' His eyes blazed. 'I must go,' he bellowed, 'I must warn the shadoor.'

"She turned pale. 'No, I forbid it. There is danger.'

" 'Do not order me to stay, Princess,' he said fiercely.

"Their eyes burned at each other. If I were to beg him as a friend or offer to go in his stead, perhaps I could keep him here, she thought. Instead, she took her ring from her finger.

" 'Take this then. It will give you entry.'

"He nodded, 'What will you do here?'

" 'I cannot tell you,' she said.

"His eyes grew cold. 'I leave tonight,' he said tersely, and turned back to the forge.

"She said nothing, but hurried away to the royal chamber. The tapestry was yet in place. 'Oh, Father, what shall I do?' she cried.

"And then the Magus came in.

" 'Heed my words,' he said quickly. 'Take the tapestry to your room. And no matter what happens, do not leave it alone there, or disorder will be loosed in the land such as there has never been.'

" 'But people will know. They will see me carrying it,' she said.

" 'Do not fear,' the Magus said. He took down the tapestry, rolled it and laid it in her arms.

"Slowly, she walked into the hall. And there, a strange sight greeted her. The people did not look at her. They did not look at anything. They were frozen in time and space. She fled to her room, put the tapestry under her bed and lay down upon it. And immediately, she fell asleep.

"It was the same dream of Gamesh and blood and water that awakened her.

" 'Go to the forge,' a voice whispered at her.

"No, I cannot leave the tapestry, she thought.

" 'Go to the forge. Your friend is in danger.'

" 'No,' she said aloud.

"And suddenly, a vision, clear and red before her, of Gamesh, bathed in blood. 'No!' she screamed and ran from her room to the forge.

" 'Gamesh,' she whispered. 'Gamesh.'

"No answer.

" 'Gamesh.' Louder.

"Still silence.

" 'Gamesh!'

"And then, a harsh voice, rough and low. 'You won't find him here, Princess.' The blacksmith appeared before her. 'He was caught on the road an hour past.'

" 'Caught . . .'

" 'Caught. And to be honored for it.'

" 'Honored . . .'

" 'Yes, Princess, truly *honored*.' He smiled through clenched teeth.

"Noura screamed and fainted.

"It was hot when she awoke. The sun baked her skin.

" 'You must dress,' someone was saying, 'for this great day.'

"Her head hurt. She could not remember. Someone helped her into her robe, her sandals, and led her outside.

"A crowd lined the path up the hill. The procession was long and slow. At its lead was Smerdis on a magnificent white horse. Something awakened in her. Then she saw Gamesh. And she remembered the tapestry she'd left beneath her bed.

"There came a cry, trumpets from somewhere, hoofbeats, then flashing swords. And Gamesh lay bleeding on the ground.

"Noura fled. Down the hill, to the palace, into her chamber. Her mother was there already, searching a chest in the room.

"Noura pushed her aside and scrambled under the bed. She pulled out the tapestry. Talliya reached for it.

"And then the magician appeared. He pointed at the tapestry. A white light shot forth from it. Then it was gone. And all was silence."

Ashtar stopped speaking. Jessica was breathing queerly. It was Jack who spoke first.

"Is that all?" he asked.

"Not quite all," Ashtar answered wryly.

"What about Tarkesh, the Horsemaster?"

"The legends say that if the messenger brings Gabdon back to him and he accepts the horse, he will rule once more."

"What happened to the kingdom?"

"It holds still."

"Holds still? What does that mean? You want us to believe in magic, but it's a lot of—" Jack stopped.

Jessica had made a small sound in her throat and put her hands to her head.

Jack turned to her. "Hey Jess, you're not going to get upset over this fairy tale stuff, are you?"

She stood up and walked past him to the door.

"Where are you going?"

She went outside and stood in the full autumn sunlight.

Stretching her arms upwards and then wrapping them around her chest, Jessica said, "Noura." The sunlight paled. The farmhouse faded. And she saw, misty and blurred, a figure holding out its arms to her.

# 14

HER TEETH were chattering and her head throbbed. She could hear Jack's distant voice calling her as she crouched down behind a rusted plow. The shed was damp. It smelled faintly of manure. She didn't care.

"Jessica!" Ashtar looked down at her. "Come!" He lifted her to her feet.

She let him lead her out of the shed.

"She would not harm you," he said. "If you go now to help, it will be easier."

Jessica stared at him and said nothing.

"You are called, Jessica. You are the Messenger. The Protector of Gabdon."

"Why me?" Jessica whispered.

Ashtar smiled and said gently, "Because it is so. Through you, worlds may meet. The order of things may change. Time and space do not rest in straight lines. They are ring upon ring. And sometimes the rings may touch and alter what may have been. I have been a traveler in those rings. Noura is now in a ring outside your time and her time to keep her safe. You can help her and her people. You can take the tapestry to Tarkesh. He must return to his people, or there will be war. Even now it may be too late.

"No!" Jessica howled. "Let me be! Let me be!"

Ashtar was silent. Then he said, "No one shall force you. But if you do not go, I give you this advice: do not let your friend or the tapestry out of your sight."

And as Jessica still stared, Ashtar raised his arms above his head, twined one wrist about the other until the palms touched and then disappeared from sight.

She reached out a hand, then dropped it and, with a sharp cry, began to run. Her sneakers kicked up tiny pebbles, clods of earth as she pelted down the road. She ran until she caught her toe in a root and fell face down. Unhurt, she drew herself onto her knees and began to pound the ground with doubled fists.

"No, no, no. What do you all want from me? I can't help any of you! I can't do anything. Why don't you all leave me alone!" She yelled until her throat was raw. Then, she sat motionless for a long time, staring into space.

When she came back to her self, it was late afternoon. Long shadows and the smell of turning leaves. It was still warm, but the night would soon bring its chill. She bent down and pulled at a weed. It exploded in her hand, scattering a handful of green seeds. She laughed, startled. Then she turned and headed back toward the farmhouse, listening to the silence broken only by the occasional call of a starling. She walked, paused, looked up at a hawk, circling slowly, then hovering. And suddenly, there was a chorus of cries as birds burst into the air around her. The hawk swooped, rose, a vole or some other rodent in its beak. It flew off. The other birds slowly settled back to their roosts. The solitary starling mewed once more. Perhaps it's never safe, she thought. She felt a surge of fear. Jack, I've got to get back to Jack.

She jumped to her feet. Something was wrong, terribly wrong. Jessica began to run. The feeling grew stronger—a cresting wave in her stomach. Faster she ran, until her breathing was jagged and her chest burned.

She sprinted up the path to the farmhouse and fell against the trough. Plunging her hands in, she splashed herself with the stinking water.

"Jack," she called hoarsely, "I'm back, I'm back." She jogged to the door and threw it open.

"No!" she shouted.

Jack was pinioned by two men, dull armor over their tunics.

Before them, the Red Lady faced Ashtar, who held the tapestry in his arms.

Jessica ran and seized it from him.

The Red Lady smiled and held out her arms.

"NO!" Jessica cried again.

"Ahhh," Jack moaned.

Jessica stared, torn, at him. His arm was twisted hard behind him. He moaned again.

"Jack . . ."

"Give me the tapestry," said the Red Lady. "And the boy is free."

Jack looked at Jessica, his eyes pleading.

She took a step toward him.

"Ashtar," she begged. "Help me!"

"I cannot now," he said.

"The tapestry," the Red Lady said.

One of the men kicked Jack's swollen ankle. He screamed in pain.

"Oh God," Jessica cried and held out the tapestry.

The Red Lady reached out her arms.

Then a rushing came into Jessica's ears. The tapestry began to glow. Voices sounded, cries mixed with the ring of steel. And everywhere was white and red.

"No!" she screamed.

In the quiet, she saw the tapestry still in her arms.

But Jack and his captors were gone.

# 15

JESSICA flung the tapestry across the room. "Why?" she cried. "Why? I shouldn't have left him. Why did I leave him?"

She felt a hand on her shoulder.

"Thus it spins," Ashtar said.

Guilt seized her. Three times she could have given the horse to the Red Lady, and three times she had refused. But then, she hadn't realized the consequences, didn't know that Jack would be the ransom. Except for this last time. Why hadn't she given them the tapestry? It must have been Ashtar who stopped her. She twisted around and struck at him. "And you! I sent a friend to God-knows-where for you—and that damned tapestry."

Ashtar said nothing.

Furiously, Jessica beat her fists at his chest. "Bring him back! Bring him back!"

"I cannot."

"Liar, liar, liar!" She sank to her knees and sobbed bitterly.

When her weeping subsided, Ashtar said, "I am sorry it has come this way. It would've been easier if you had gone before. Now it takes this turning. Listen to me, Jessica. I cannot bring your friend back, but there is a way for you."

"A way . . ."

"Yes, Gabdon will guide you."

"Gabdon," she spat out. "The devil created him."

"Perhaps, but I doubt it. However, we have little time to discuss theology. Do you want to save your friend?"

She looked at him fiercely. "I would give my life to save Jack."

"Let us hope that is not necessary. Now, take up the tapestry, unroll it and call the name."

"And then . . ."

"The veil will part."

"The veil?"

"You shall see."

"Why should I believe you?"

"Because you have no other choice," Ashtar answered.

Jessica stood still a moment. Then she said, "So you win. You all win."

Forgetting her knapsack in the corner, she walked slowly across the room and picked up the tapestry. Her fingers tingled, and her breath came short. She carried the tapestry outside into the waning sunlight. Carefully, she unrolled it. The red, gold and silver leaped at her as they never had before. She stared at the white star on the horse's forehead. She took a deep breath. Then she called, "Gabdon!"

White and thunder. And once again, Gabdon reared before her. And once again, the implacable eyes searched her face.

She climbed on, and Ashtar climbed on behind her. She gripped the reins tightly. "Now!" she said. But the horse did not move.

"He waits," Ashtar said.

"For what?"

"For your trust."

"I do not understand." But she did. There was terror in her chest, tightness in her throat. She feared the great beast and where he would take her. And she could not master the horse until she mastered her fear.

Finally, she asked, "What can I do?"

"Think on him as he is: powerful, yes, but also a horse, a beast without malice."

She dropped the reins, put out her hand and touched the mane. Further. The neck. Warm, pulsing. She bent low, stretched out her arm, touched the star. And suddenly she felt as if three worlds had joined—her world, the world of the horse and something else, large and unseen. Gabdon seemed to sense it too, for he whinnied gently, and nodded his head. Her heart felt full, and she smiled, while great tears coursed down her cheeks. "Good Gabdon," she said. "Good, good Gabdon." He whinnied once more, and then he began to run.

The colors of the fields, the leaves, the sky grew dimmer and dimmer. She felt as though she were moving through water. Something dark, amorphous appeared in the distance, grew larger, loomed. She opened her mouth, but no sound came. And then, they entered the dark.

Years, centuries, perhaps light years, passed; gray shapes brushed her head and shoulders. Terrified, she buried her face in Gabdon's neck and breathed deeply his animal smell.

Then, all at once, colors flamed with a brilliance that hurt her eyes. Scarlet birds, golden sky, silver sands below. Gabdon slowed, slowed, set down softly on the sand.

With Ashtar at her side, she dismounted, stood erect and surveyed the desert around her. "Home?" she said.

"Home." Ashtar nodded.

# 16

SHE HAS come. I see her when the Magus—for I suspect it is he—so allows me: yet distant, yet out of reach. Still, an invisible cord binds us one to the other as though we were kin. I long to sit near her, to link fingers like sisters, to speak to her of Gamesh, for I sense she would understand. She too has a friend; she has several times murmured his name, and like rods of light, her words appeared to me. Would I could answer.

I did speak to her once when she called out my name. And she heard, but then turned in fear. She is not a willing Messenger. But she is the Messenger nonetheless. And so brave and strong. Would that I could learn courage from her!

When it is done, my people will bless her. My poor people. They are not stupid, not shiftless, not flighty, not vain. But they are frightened and confused. They need one to guide and teach. When my father is Horsemaster once more, he will help them know their own hearts. And I will live among them, nursing the old and the young and the sick, for such is the choice I have made. I can do nothing for my people shut up in my palace or in this gray place. When I am free once more, I will wear the simple robe. I will wear the leather sandals. I will travel from village to village with a light heart. Then perhaps I may gather the ma-lat and let it fill me.

If the Messenger loved my people as I do, perhaps she would be more willing. But she knows them not. Oh, if I could speak to her again and be heard, I would instruct her in their ways. And I would try to soothe her rage. For there is in her a fury that burns almost as bright as the ma-lat, though with a different light: it will eat at her heart until her breast will be as hollow as that of my mother. Oh, Magus, let me speak with the Messenger. Let there be commerce between us that together we may bring Gabdon to my father and fear not my mother.

What is this I speak? What have I to do with the Messenger? I am weak. She is strong. I can do nothing. And the Red Lady stirs. I can feel her power growing. She has waited, as I wait; but in her stillness, her power, bent upon itself, has doubled like a twin-headed snake that spits venom into the eyes of its prey. I pray the Messenger will not be blinded. She will need all of her ma-lat, all of her heart. Would I could lend her what little there is of my own! Oh, Magus, give me back my tongue. Let me not be so alone!

# 17

"AGAIN."

"I can't."

"Again."

Jessica sighed, slung her right leg wearily across the donkey's broad back and tried to pull herself upright, but she slipped and fell heavily to the ground.

"I don't understand. I was able to ride Gabdon even though I'd never been on a horse before, but I can't for the life of me get on this donkey."

"You will learn," Ashtar said. "Now, again."

"No."

"Again."

Then she began to shout, "No! This is ridiculous. I've been in this godforsaken place for a week, while Jack is . . . God knows where he is! And you keep insisting I learn to ride a donkey, learn to pack a donkey, learn to build a fire, learn to put out a fire, learn to speak the language, learn to do everything except rescue Jack!"

Ashtar said nothing. Jessica glared at him, but when he stared back impassively, she lowered her eyes. They'd been through all this days ago, when they'd first arrived at the house where Ashtar had dwelled for many years until summoned by the Law of Al-tonah. A three days' ride from the Imperial City. If she called Gabdon, they could be there in three minutes. And she wanted to call Gabdon, to feel his warm, strong back beneath her, to be one with his world. But Ashtar had said if they arrived on the horse, the alarm would be raised; then Smerdis and his army would seize Gabdon and all would be lost.

"I don't care about Gabdon," Jessica had shouted. But the moment she said the words, she knew they weren't true. She had ridden the horse. And having ridden him, she could not forget him. He was the essence of power and beauty. Neither goodness nor evil was part of him: he could be used for either purpose. She did not want him used for evil; she hated the thought of his being held captive by some master who would use him to enslave a people, to hold a nation in his fist. But it was Jack she had to help. Jack came first, even if it meant Gabdon or Tarkesh or Noura or this whole kingdom, wherever it was, were to fall. "I don't care about Gabdon. I have to find Jack."

"Do you wish to find him only to lose him?" Ashtar had said quietly.

Jessica fell silent and listened.

"Wherever the boy is, he is safe. The Red Lady would not kill so valuable a prize, at least not until the tapestry is in her hands. And she will make certain that you know where he is, in her own good time, so that you will, as you might say, 'play into her hands.' That is why we must be one step ahead of her.

And that is why, when you play into her hands, you must make sure to have a dagger in your own."

She had looked at him, wide-eyed, and swallowed hard. "I will," she had answered. "I will."

And then he had explained that she was to become a merchant's daughter, sun-baked and diffident, a nomad used to the harsh, baked life of the desert. In this guise she could travel in safety and find Jack.

So she was trying, trying hard, but she was growing more and more impatient; the task seemed nearly impossible.

Tears welled in her eyes, but she clenched her fists and fought them away.

"How are your feet?" Ashtar asked kindly.

She glanced at them, mottled with patches of peeling skin, and wiggled her toes. Sullenly, she answered, "Better."

"Do you need more ointment?"

"Maybe a little," she said reluctantly.

He nodded and fetched a jar. He knelt down and examined the burns. "Yes, they are healing. Soon, you will be brown as a camhi nut." Deftly, Ashtar poured ointment into his palm and smoothed it over her feet. "Ah, you are making calluses on your heels. That is very good. You will be ready to travel in another week or so."

"Another week—" Jessica started to say, but she bit off the words. After all, what was the use? They would leave when Ashtar decreed it, and not before.

"Now, stand up, daughter, and try to take poor old Moofta for a ride," Ashtar said, patting her ankle.

She sighed once more and stood. Slowly, she approached the donkey. "What am I doing wrong?" she said.

And then, as though someone had lit a candle in her head, a voice said, "Throw your arms around his neck."

She obeyed, pulled herself up and over, and soon she was digging her heels softly into Moofta's fat sides and riding him slowly around the house.

"I did it! I did it!" she cheered as she turned the corner to greet Ashtar. And the voice in her head laughed and wept with her.

# 18

THE SECOND week passed almost as slowly as the first, but now Jessica was feeling a little more pleased with herself. She had learned to cook simple meals, to feed the kiln, to gather figs. She was becoming adept at gauging the weather, at mending a robe, at speaking a new language. And when she faltered, Noura spoke: teaching, correcting, guiding. Well, perhaps "spoke" was the wrong word. To Jessica, Noura's words were like pinpoints of light. But she grew used to this "speech"; she welcomed it. Noura was patient, accepting, soothing. Though sometimes Jessica did resent the thought that all this was done to save a kingdom, and not to save Jack.

One morning, Jessica was idly inspecting herself for the fleas that poor Moofta inevitably gave her and wishing she could have a bath, when Ashtar said, "So, daughter, are you ready today for a 'dress rehearsal'?" He smiled as he said the last words.

She looked at him in surprise. He was shaping a clay pot in his hands on a small stone wheel. She watched the form spin, narrow and flesh out.

"If you think I'm ready," she said.

"Do you think you are?"

"I hope so."

"Good."

They sat in silence for a time, and then Jessica asked, "Ashtar, why don't you use magic to make pots?"

Still manipulating the vessel, Ashtar answered sternly, "Magic is a large thing—it governs all of us, just as we govern it. One does not use what you call magic frivolously. There is an ancient proverb that says, 'If your two hands will do, use them.' One should not seek for too many short-cuts. Especially where power is concerned."

"I don't understand," Jessica said. "How does magic govern all of us and how do we govern magic?"

Ashtar smiled. "Ah, a good question." He paused, then answered slowly, "There is one power, or force you may call it, that flows through all of us, and we are all representatives of that power. If we work to gather that power, we can use it well or we can use it ill. Or we can pretend the power does not exist. The last is a thing many chose to do through fear, through laziness, through ignorance. But just because they do not choose to recognize the power does not mean the power is not there. It is there, albeit unfocused. It is everpresent in everyone and everything throughout the concentric circles of time and space. Here we have a word for this power. We call it the ma-lat. You may come across that word. Now you will know what it means."

As Ashtar completed the pot and set it to dry before being fired in the kiln, Jessica thought over what he had said. Ma-lat.

"Go and feed the kiln, daughter," Ashtar said. "Soon it will be time to see if you have learned your lessons well."

Jessica bowed slightly, the way he had taught her, and went out to the kiln.

THE BROWN-SKINNED girl in the long, roughly woven tunic and loose trousers held out a narrow-mouthed white clay jug for the inspection of the customer, a friendly postal carrier.

"Hmmm. Nice workmanship. You must keep a hot kiln," he said slyly to the girl.

She stared boldly at him until Noura's voice whispered, "Do not be forward with him," and she lowered her eyes discreetly.

The postal carrier cleared his throat and turned to the old man standing next to the girl. "I have never seen you merchants before. Trying a new route?"

"Yes," he replied. "One gets tired of old ways."

"Wise words, old man. And the very sentiments I hold. I say, extend those sentiments to kingship!"

"You feel we need a new shadoor?"

"You are very quick. Yes, I believe it is time for a change. And you?"

Ashtar smiled, but said nothing. The carrier took his smile for assent, and clapped him on the back.

"Well, I must be on my way. Must reach Medwar by tomorrow morning. I carry a letter for the Emir Fatoosh. Anything you want delivered there? No? Well, here is good fortune to you. And to your beautiful daughter. May you marry her well." The postal carrier paid for the jug, packed it on his horse, mounted and rode away.

The old man turned to his daughter. "Congratulations. You have studied well. As you would say in your country, you have 'passed the test.' "

She nearly flung her arms around him.

"A little talent and a little help from my friends," she said, with a laugh. In her head she could hear Noura laugh, too.

"You will need both. We have, as you would say, 'not made it yet.' "

She grew serious. "No. But we will. We must."

"Yes, Jessica," Ashtar replied, "we must. Tonight we will leave for the Imperial City. And the real test will begin."

NIGHT SLID across the desert. The asses stood tied outside the small stone house. Inside, firelit, Jessica dipped her fingers in a bowl and brought them, dripping, to her lips. The food tasted better than any dish she could remember.

Then, Ashtar rose. "It is time to leave," he said.

Together they packed a small tent, provisions and their wares on one donkey. Under a rug on Moofta, the lead donkey, was the tapestry of Gabdon. Ashtar tied the reins with a long rope to Moofta and the two mounted him.

The air was surprisingly cold, and Jessica was grateful for the blanket around her shoulders.

Ashtar looked once more on his house. "I bid you well, stones," he said. "Grant I may see you once more."

Jessica said nothing.

They rode quietly, neither desiring to talk, across the sands that now stretched silver as far as one could see beneath a pale moon.

Jessica thought about Jack. The men had been so brutal. Dear God, they weren't still beating him, were they? Were they caring for his ankle? Were they feeding him? Each question pierced her like a needle.

So enmeshed was she in her thoughts that she did not see the figure on the horse who rose from the sand, until the rope lashed around her waist and threw her to the ground.

"Stand," the figure commanded, "and come with me."

She stumbled to her feet, Ashtar following beside her.

The man led them west over small dunes to a string of tents. They entered one and stood before another man, obviously an officer, large and bearded, wearing armor and holding a torch.

"Who are you who rides unbidden through the land of Smerdis?" he bellowed.

"Of Tarkesh," Jessica growled before she could stop herself.

Ashtar gripped her arm.

An angry murmur escaped the man with the whip. The officer silenced him. "So, you are friends of Tarkesh," he said.

"No, we are not friends of Tarkesh," Ashtar spoke. "We understood this to be the kingdom of Tarkesh."

"You are wrong. This is the kingdom of Smerdis."

Ashtar and Jessica said nothing.

"Do you swear allegiance to him who is our shadoor?"

"We can swear allegiance to no one. We are not from this land."

"From where do you come?"

"From Dakara."

"And you are heading where?"

"On the Kadmar route to sell our wares."

"Inspect them, Linan."

Ashtar bid Jessica unpack the pottery. Carefully she did so. White the officer looked on, the soldier, Linan, inspected every piece.

"What else have you here?" he questioned.

"Merely our household provisions."

Linan glanced up at the officer, who nodded, then he said, "Let me see them."

Jessica took down the water bags, the tent, the rugs from the donkey. The soldier scrutinized everything. Then he pointed to the second donkey. Jessica lifted off several rugs, exposing the folded tapestry.

"What is this?"

"Just another small rug."

"Unfold it."

Jessica's chest tightened.

"It is fragile," Ashtar said. Jessica heard desperation in his voice.

"I order you to show it to me!"

"No," she said.

Linan drew his sword.

"Hold," the officer said. Then he stood close to Jessica, picked up her chin with his hand and shone the torch full in her face. The light blinded her, and she could not see his reaction. But then he put aside the torch and said, "That will be all, Linan. You have done well. You merchants, pack your things and leave."

Jessica did not understand what had just transpired, but she breathed deeply, bowed and quickly helped Ashtar pack the donkey once again. She hoped for Noura's voice and comfort, but it did not come. The officer watched them unwaveringly. Jessica could feel his gaze burning her back. Finally, they were ready; they mounted Moofta and turned him in the direction of the Imperial City.

Then the officer called to them, his voice low and calm, but full of an emotion Jessica could not name. "If you are stopped again, tell them you have seen Qajar of Fendi," he said, "and he has vouched for you upon the head of his mother." Immediately he turned and went back inside the tent.

Jessica did not ask Ashtar what the man had meant, for she understood: they were being given license to travel the desert in safety from Smerdis's men. But Smerdis and his men were not the only beings from whom Jessica needed protection. She knew that only too well.

# 19

THE REST of their night journey was peaceful. In the early morning, when the sun rose fiery, they stopped, took the tapestry and a few supplies from the donkeys, pitched their small tent and breakfasted.

All was calm, hot and heavy. Jessica fidgeted and fanned her face. Ashtar offered her a drink and then began to make polite conversation. "Well, my child, how do you like being a merchant's daughter?" he said.

"It's not so bad, except for the heat," Jessica said, trying to raise one eyebrow the way Ashtar could.

"Do you miss your parents?"

She felt herself stiffen. "Why do you ask?"

"I believe it is normal to be homesick."

"I miss my home," she said cautiously.

"But not your parents?"

"My mother and I don't get along too well. And my father . . . my father left a long time ago," she answered curtly, hoping he'd drop the subject.

But he didn't. "Why did your father leave?"

"I don't know why," she said, more sharply than she'd intended. "He didn't give me any reasons . . . Anyway, why are you asking me all this?"

Ashtar rested his chin in his hand. "You remind me of a strange animal I once saw in my travels. It moved quickly, and it grew long spines right out of its back. When anything came near, it rolled into a ball and said, 'Keep away.' "

"A porcupine," Jessica murmured. "A prickly porcupine."

Then she shook her head and said angrily, "What a stupid comparison."

"Be calm, daughter," Ashtar said. "It is not wise to expend too much energy in such heat."

She glared at him and forced herself to take a long, deep breath. When she relaxed, she remembered a question that was puzzling her. "Ashtar, the Red Lady knows I bear Gabdon, but does Tarkesh?"

"Yes, he knows."

"Did you tell him?"

"In a way."

"In a dream," Jessica responded.

Ashtar smiled again.

Then Jessica asked, "Ashtar, do you know why Noura has not spoken to me in two days?"

Ashtar frowned. "I am not certain," he said. "I shall try to find out."

And Jessica knew she would get no further answers from him.

Presently, they retired.

"Sleep, my daughter," Ashtar said. "And may you dream of rivers."

She thought sleep would not come, but it descended, as inexorably as the sun and the heat rose.

She did not dream of rivers, nor of Noura or Gabdon or Jack or the Red Lady. Instead, she dreamed of her father.

He stood before her, just the way he had looked when she was five. "Well, Jesse James," he said. "You still quick on the trigger?"

It was their old private joke.

"Yeth, thir," she lisped in a little girl voice, pulling out an imaginary gun.

Somewhere behind her, she heard her mother's voice say, "You want to make her a fighter, like you, Frank?"

His face sagged. "I'm not much of a fighter, Adrienne. I give up too fast. Not like Jess. Right, Jesse James?"

"Yeth, thir," she answered. She looked down at the imaginary gun. It had become real. She didn't blink when she pulled the trigger.

It was a strange, hollow whirring that awakened her, a whirring that grew steadily louder.

She sat up. Ashtar was not in the tent. She called his name. There was no response.

She rose and left the tent. No Ashtar. But there, on the horizon, a yellow mass. Rolling. Nearing. The mass became a high, opaque wall.

"Ashtar," she shouted. "Ashtar!"

A blast of burning air. Then a sinister calm. The wall was still nearer.

"Ashtar!"

Suddenly, the whirring wind burst, driving sand into her eyes, her nose, her mouth, stopping up her scream. She could no longer walk.

The donkeys brayed and sank to the sand.

Jessica dropped down and crawled toward the tent.

*I'm going to be buried alive*, she thought, and then she remembered Gabdon.

She could hardly see the tent flap, fluttering wildly in the wind.

She pulled herself into the tent. It billowed madly, threatening to collapse upon her as the wind and sand beat against it. *Gabdon, dear Gabdon*, she thought. *I can't give you to the wind.* She reached under the pile of rugs and dragged out the tapestry. With it came a length of rope. Fighting against the waving walls, she flung the tapestry on her back and passed the rope around it, over and under her arms, and pulled it tight.

Then, with a crack, the tent poles broke. The tent skin rent, hung momentarily in the air, and then disappeared to the wind.

*Dorothy and Kansas*, Jessica thought and then laughed hysterically until the sand made her choke.

She crouched, blind, on the sand, her hands before her, groping for a rock, a bush. Then she thought of the donkeys. If she found them she'd be safe. She stumbled on. Rough hair. Her hands touched rough hair. A donkey. Crouching blind, she pulled herself over to the beast, reached, crawled around it. Again her hands touched hair. The two donkeys, side by side, kneeling, dumbly awaiting their fate.

She lay between them. Low. Breathing into their musky sides.

*I will wait too*, she thought.

And the wind, the heat roared on.

# 20

I HAD a dream. That is how I must describe it, although I do not seem to sleep in this place in time out of time. But what else could it have been? I saw Gamesh before me, pale and thin, lying on gray stones. But when I called his name, he did not look up; he did not answer. And I, at last, shedding my royal bearing, began to weep.

Oh, I curse the last moon, when my mother spread her poison over us all. Gamesh and I did not speak, did not love. And when I learned he had spoken true it was too late. There was a day— a night—ere my father departed that is so dear to my heart. The night of Bish-a-em, blessing of waters. The priestesses had danced the solemn nabala and then, equally solemn, we waded into the river—Mother, Father, Smerdis and I. We stood quiet, then raised our hands to the people to join us. Representatives from all households did so, slow, stately. Then we sang the song of praise to Bodar, moving gently from one foot to the other until the High Priestess said, "Be free, my children, free as the river. Flow to one another in peace and joy!" A great shout rose, and the people rushed into one another's arms. I was expected to choose a son of the Nishra family; but then—and only then—

I defied convention and my mother's wrath and chose Gamesh instead. I grabbed his hand, and his eyes opened full and wide as we ran downstream to the Grove of Frena.

"Why do you choose this unworthy servant, handmaiden of Bodar," Gamesh said, speaking the prescribed words.

I was to answer, "Worthy and unworthy join as one under the aegis of the goddess." But what I said was, "Because you are my friend and my love."

Gamesh was shocked. "Oh, Noura. Do not . . . do not . . ." he stammered.

And then I pressed my lips to his. He sighed, and our bodies entwined. It was brief. Too brief. The priestesses came to gather us, to escort us back to the palace, but I did not want to leave the Grove of Frena nor Gamesh's arms. It was then I swore to marry him, though I said not the words aloud.

Oh, Magus, why have I had this dream? The pain comes afresh and bitter are the tears that stain my cheeks. Neither grief nor guilt will bring Gamesh to me, yet guilty and grief-stricken I am. Who has sent this dream? Was it you, or could it be the voice that whispers? It is faint, this voice, but it murmurs of betrayal and doubt. I try to stop my ears, but it is inside my skull and I cannot blot it out. It grows hard to hear the Messenger. Harder still to speak. I will need all my poor strength to help her. I will need all my poor strength and more to stop from going mad.

# 21

THE WIND was gone. The sullen heat remained. And the sand was still, here flat, there pushed into a huge dune, but still.

Jessica stood between the two donkeys, who were shaking their sides and snorting sand from their nostrils. The tapestry felt heavy on her back.

*I am not dead, have not been buried,* she thought. "I am alive!" she called defiantly to the sun. "Do you hear me? I am alive, and Gabdon is safe!"

She put her hands to her face, pitted with sand. *Over that dune. I will go to the top of that dune and I will know.*

She unstrapped the tapestry, and tied it to a donkey. Then she tied the donkeys together, mounted and rode slowly. Her eyes searched for a bush or the remnants of the tent or a small brown man in a long robe. But there was only the sand.

The dune grew before her, a crumbling, but implacable pyramid.

The donkeys trod steadily, hoof after hoof.

*When I reach the top, . . . There!*

The donkeys paused.

The top was beneath her.

And below, the desert slanted away, mile upon sand-stormed mile, marked only by other dunes identical to the one on which she stood.

"Ashtar," she cried, "Ashtar! Ashtar!"

And then, she began to laugh. Shards of laughter that tore at her throat. She threw herself down and clawed the sand. Dug and dug. And laughed.

Abruptly, the sharp laughter ceased. She stopped digging.

"I will not go mad," she said. "I will summon Gabdon. We will ride to the Imperial City and rescue Jack and everything else can go to hell." She felt as though she were some sort of robot as she went through the mechanical motions of taking down and unwrapping the tapestry. Then, she called the horse to her.

He came, cantering over the dune, and blew his warm breath into her hair. She turned her head because she did not want to look into his eyes and noticed the two donkeys. The poor beasts had jumped back, staring and braying at the horse, until they realized that Gabdon was not going to hurt them. They would

die without food or water, she thought, They needed someone to care for them. Then she shook her head. No, they were
desert animals; they could take care of themselves. Couldn't
they, Gabdon?

Forgetting her intention, she looked into the horse's eyes.
This time they were not implacable, but deep and limpid. She
felt herself falling into them. Falling softly, weightlessly. Colors
flashed before her—blue, green, violet, red, yellow, white. A
nebula of pure white light, tunneling, spiraling, becoming two
serpents entwined, one upon the other. She became frightened.
Not of the serpents, but of the growing power she felt stirring
and rising within herself. "No . . . not now . . . not me!" she cried
out. The serpents flickered, reformed, a nebula once more. "No
. . . I . . . have to save . . . Jack . . . have to," she yelled. "Gabdon
. . . take me to . . ." But she could not get the words out. She
reached forward and touched the horse's flank.

"My dear friend," she whispered. "Agdosh!" The nebula
vanished. The horse blinked. Jessica stood still. *Forgive me,
Jack. Forgive me, Gabdon. Forgive me.* She pressed her head
against the horse's neck. He nuzzled her gently. She felt terribly, hugely sad, but somehow stronger. She took a deep breath,
seized the tapestry and wrapped it up tightly. "Agdosh!" she
said again, this time, clearly and firmly. And Gabdon disappeared. Then she turned to the donkeys. The waterbags were
still hanging from the saddle of rugs. She shook them.

*Enough for at least another day—until we reach the oasis,
wherever that is,* she thought.

She allowed herself a small drink, the donkeys a larger share.
*Ashtar is gone,* she thought. *He might be dead or alive. If
he is alive, he will find me. If he is dead* . . . She licked her
cracked lips and sighed. "We will ride to the next dune," she
announced.

Resolutely, she fastened the tapestry to a donkey, mounted
once more and shook her fist at the sky. "You have not won."

*I have not won yet,* the sun answered, and laughed, a sound
like a hundred bleached bones clicking.

"Go," she shouted to the donkey and they pressed on.

The next dune was not far, but it was higher than the last. Once the lead donkey stumbled.

"The sand is soft, but not merciful, my friend," Jessica said, and then thought, *I am beginning to sound like Ashtar. Perhaps it is the climate.*

The donkeys moved carefully on, and Jessica closed her eyes to the brutal sun.

At last they reached the summit. Only then did she open her eyes. And what she saw made her gasp.

Below were several scrubby trees, a camel, and two tents, blossoming blue and red in the hot yellow sand.

"Quick," she shouted to the lead donkey, thrusting her heels into its side.

Sliding. Down the side of the dune. *Please, let it be real and not a mirage,* she prayed, and begged the donkey to hurry.

And then, she was before the first tent.

"Hello," she called. "Is someone there?"

She dismounted, staggered toward the tent.

"Please. Someone. Help me."

She reached for the flap, pulled it aside.

"Hello . . ."

Then, cold and bright against her aching throat, the knife gleamed. She tensed to receive the pain. But the steel did not cut.

"Kill her and have done, Komar," said an impatient female voice behind her.

"No," said the man who was called Komar. "I think not."

"Kill her, you fool, she will only bring trouble."

But the knife lowered and the hand that held it spun Jessica around.

For the first time, she saw her captor, and she was startled by how handsome he was: his mouth full and soft, his eyes large and cunning.

But his voice was cruel. "Who are you?" he demanded.

"Jessica," she answered.

"You lie. There is no such name as that."

"All right then," she spat back. "It is Noura."

He slapped her. "Do not dare to mock me."

"I tell you she'll be nothing but trouble," the small, dark woman beside him snapped.

"She will cause *me* no trouble. Now, tell me, once more, who are you?"

Jessica's courage left her. They will surely kill me, or worse, throw me back to the sands. Think. History. Ancient names. Please God, help me . . .

And then, Noura's voice said, "Vashti."

*Oh, Noura, why did you leave me for days. I thought you were hurt. Or that you too had deserted me,* Jessica cried out silently.

"I will never desert you," Noura answered, but her voice was faint and hesistant.

Jessica clenched her fists and looked into Komar's eyes. "I am called Vashti," she said through her teeth.

Komar smiled. "That is better," he said. "Vashti. Little Vashti." He whistled a snatch of an odd, spiraling tune. Then, his voice grew lower, cajoling. "Tell me, little Vashti, do you know how to steal?"

Jessica stared, mouth agape.

Komar laughed. "Well, little Vashti, well, it does not matter. You will learn. You will certainly learn."

# 22

SHE LAY on a tattered rug surrounded by an astounding assortment of riches: silver pitchers, piles of bracelets, necklaces, rings encrusted with brilliant stones, fine woven rugs, bronze caskets of sweetmeats, cloisonne jugs of rich wine.

The small, dark woman sat scowling at her. "He said to bring you water and figs." She shoved a waterskin and a copper bowl toward Jessica.

*I should refuse them. Not eat or drink. Perhaps then they'd be forced to let me go,* she thought. *But no, they'd just leave me to starve.*

She sighed and reached for the skin, brought it to her cracked lips and drank greedily.

"You cost us much water. Your donkeys deserve it more than you," the dark woman snarled. "You had better make a good thief."

"The donkeys," Jessica gasped, remembering the tapestry strapped to Moofta's back. "Are they all right?"

The woman looked at her strangely. "Of course they are all right. Asses are more valuable than stupid girls."

Jessica said nothing. It was best not to seem too concerned. She felt certain now that they had not inspected the dirty rug on the donkey's back. Slowly, she began to eat the figs.

The woman laid a hand on her rounded stomach.

"Zaka," she swore. Then she turned to a pile of jewelry and began sorting it, tossing the copper and brass bangles into one heap, carefully examining gold and silver bejeweled pieces and wrapping these in silk scarves.

"Where did you get those?" Jessica asked.

The woman only muttered another curse and continued to work.

Jessica heard whistling, and then the tent flap opened and Komar entered. "Ah, Peri, already at work," he said, with a smile. "And little Vashti, you too will soon start work."

Emboldened by his manner, Jessica asked, "Komar, where did all of this come from?"

Peri growled again, but Komar told her to be quiet. "Since you are to be one of us, you have a right to ask. These riches came from a caravan bearing them as gifts to the new shadoor."

Jessica did not want to make the mistake she had before, so she asked, "Shadoor Smerdis?"

"Yes, Smerdis, of course. Our shadoor."

"No, not mine. I come from Dakara."

"Ah, Dakara. A lovely place. And full of gold. Right, Peri?"
He laughed sardonically, and Peri joined in with him.

Jessica decided to probe delicately. "But he is not the shadoor
yet, is he? Smerdis, I mean."

Komar stopped laughing abruptly. "No, not yet, but as good
as it. He is a vain, stupid man, and I shall be delighted when
we—" Peri gripped his arm. He paused, and then said to her,
"Yes, you are right. Perhaps she is not yet ready for that bit of
information."

*They hate Smerdis. They must support Tarkesh.* Jessica felt
a wave of fear and hope rise in her, but she quickly pushed it
down. *They might care as little for Tarkesh as for Smerdis. I
must take care, go one step at a time, if I'm to see Jack again,*
she thought. She was wondering how to find out more about
their feelings, when Komar came near and fixing his eyes on
her said, "And now, little Vashti, it is time to make you more
beautiful than you already are."

He unwound the turban she wore from her head and, loosing
her thick, brown hair, ran his hand through it.

She shivered and drew back.

"Good," he said. "So young she does not have to be taught
shyness."

She winced at his words, and he laughed.

"Peri, comb and perfume her hair. Tonight, she will be a
dancing girl."

Jessica's hand flew to her mouth.

"Do not be so shocked, little Vashti. You will not have to
dance. Medwar Village is but half an evening's ride from here.
There is a merchant of sorts who is once again home from his
travels and who looks for such maidens to buy and sell to the
emir. You will be bought."

Jessica sat still, looking at that beautiful full mouth speaking
such horrible words, and wondered at the falseness of mere
appearances. A little cry escaped her.

"Ah, she cries. But, little Vashti, you will not remain sold.
For you see, this merchant buys not only dancing girls, but bolts

of silk in most rare and wondrous colors. You will find his store-room, hand his silk out the window to Peri and myself and then climb out the same window to our waiting arms."

Aghast, she trembled and still said nothing.

"You will find the life of a thief no worse than that of—

"No," she said.

He cocked his head and smiled. "No? I think yes, my pretty Vashti."

"No," she said, louder this time.

"I told you she'd bring nothing but trouble. Kill her now, Komar," Peri snapped.

But Komar ignored her. He smiled again and said in a honey-eyed voice, "Do you know what disembowelment means, little Vashti?"

"Yes," Jessica said, "and the answer is still no."

Komar pulled out his knife and pressed it against her stomach. Then, a thought came to her.

"Unless . . ." she said quickly.

He eased his grip on the knife. "Unless?"

"Komar," she spoke clearly, firmly, "you have not left this spot today. Therefore you have spies, people who let you know when a caravan is coming or when a merchant has returned."

He smiled, this time in admiration. "You are clever. Go on. Tell me what it is you bargain for."

"I want to know something. If you will have your spies find it out for me, I will enter the merchant's house and hand his silk to you."

"Do not listen to her, Komar. She is trying to trick you," Peri shouted.

"What is it you wish to know?" he asked.

"Just this: was a boy, a stranger, brought recently to the Shadoor's palace, and is he well?"

"Is this a friend of yours from Dakara?"

"Not Dakara. Further . . . west."

Komar withdrew the knife and thrust it back in his belt. "I will have the information for you tonight—when you climb out the window after the silk."

They looked at each other for a long moment.

"I was right; you will be a good thief," he said.

"Perhaps," Jessica answered. *Perhaps I'll have to be*, she thought.

# 23

THE MAGUS has left me. And announced his leaving. Like a shadow he came to tell me he would not be able to come again. "You are in danger. I have tried to keep you safe, but I can do so no more. The Red Lady is strong. She will break you if you let her. Do not let her," he said. Then he vanished.

The Red Lady. My mother who once was. Though I fear her, I still cannot believe she would harm me. I am no threat to her. And I am of her flesh. Why should she wish to break me?

And yet, I hear her voice—for it is her—beating in my skull like Kishnan rumbling the skies with his staff of silver, his drum of iron. She speaks fear, and it fills me with trembling. She says if I help the Messenger, we will both die. But if I do not help the Messenger, I believe we shall die anyway. And my father will be destroyed in the battle that comes. My mother's voice tells me my father has destroyed himself. He is weak. Weak as his daughter. Not fit to rule. He deserted his people, and he deserted his children. But she lies. I know not why he departed, but there must be a reason. He did leave me and his people, but not for lack of love. This I know, and that I will see him again and be enfolded in his arms. He will return stronger than before. And to this, the Messenger and I will help him. To think this gives me strength to beat down my mother's voice. But only for a time. For she is strong, and I am weak. And the Messenger is no nearer to my father. I want to remind her of her duty, but it is her friend she goes first to save, and for that, I forgive her. Something in my heart knows that a friend is of more worth than a kingdom. A weakness perhaps, but a glorious weakness. My mother knows that weakness in me, too. She has preyed on it in me; she preys on it in the Messenger. And yet, and yet, perhaps in that weakness is a power. A power so strong that on it the Red Lady will be broken. I do not know, but I feel . . .

# 24

"PUT DOWN your hands, stupid girl," Peri snapped, a dripping cloth in her hand. "You are covered with grit."

Jessica remained with her arms crossed about her bare breasts. The woman had snatched off her robe before she could stop her, and naked, she had leaped to her feet.

"I will wash myself," she replied tensely.

"As you wish," Peri growled, pitching the wet rag at Jessica. Jessica caught it and began to scrub her face and neck.

"Not so hard," Peri said. "You'll take off your pretty hide."

She ignored the comment and rubbed harder, trying to force the desert to leave her skin. When she finished, she dropped the rag and demanded clothing. She was ill prepared for the splendid silken garments Peri held before her. Pale yellow trousers, tight at the ankle, billowing at the hip. A sheer flowing skirt of deep blue flecked with gold, bound at the waist with a golden girdle. A snug blue jacket that had buttons of gold. And blue, gold-traced slippers with strange toes that turned up. She struggled into the garments, shunning Peri's hands and ignoring her gruff admonitions about abuse of the fine cloth. On her ankles and wrists she wore bands hung with a myriad of tiny golden bells; about her neck were fine golden chains.

"Here's the last of it." Peri glowered, holding out a pair of large, delicate earrings, flowers etched on their flat, golden planes.

Jessica took them, then shook her head. "Not these," she said.

"Why not these? Are they not fine enough for the dancing girl?" Peri asked with a sneer.

"I cannot wear them," Jessica said curtly.

"Put in the earrings, or I will kill you myself," Peri screeched, brandishing a short, exceedingly sharp dagger.

Jessica tried to shrink back, but Peri grabbed her by the ears, knocking her off balance and tumbling them both to the floor. "Oh, Noura," Jessica called, "What do I do now." But Noura was silent. Peri sat up abruptly.

"By Golgon, what strange child are you to have unpierced ears!" she said.

Jessica did not answer.

Frightened, as though Jessica were possessed by some demon to be exorcised, Peri frowned and said, "There is only one thing to do. Wait here." And she hurriedly left the tent.

*As if I have any place to go,* Jessica thought bitterly. She touched her ears. "Betrayers," she whispered. Then, "Too late to return. Too late. Only time to turn. Thus it spins . . ." She felt glazed, numb, as though she could do nothing but stare ahead.

When Peri reentered with wine and insisted that she drink, she drank.

When Peri wrapped a white cloth about her neck, she sat quietly.

When humming Komar entered with something long, pointed and flashing silver, she could only look dully at him.

Peri took the silver thing from his hands.

"Is she drunk?" he asked.

"Let us hope so," she answered.

"No, I am not drunk," Jessica wanted to reply, but her mouth would not form the words.

"Leave now," Peri ordered Komar.

"But I want to see—"

"Leave! This is woman's work."

He did not argue, but turned and went.

"This will not take long," Peri was saying, "I cannot understand how this can be."

"Not . . . take . . . long," Jessica heard, feeling as though her head were under water.

Peri was dabbing something cool and sweet-smelling on her earlobes.

"Look at me. Are the customs in Dakara so different?"

Jessica stared into Peri's face. She smelled strongly of spice. Spice and lentils. Like soup her mother sometimes made. Jessica suddenly wanted to laugh.

Then she saw the gleaming needle in Peri's hand. And at once the numbness departed.

"No!" she screamed, trying to rise.

"Be quiet. It will not hurt long. A dancing girl must wear earrings."

"No!" she cried again, pushing hard at Peri's wrist. "Noura! Ashtar! Someone help me!"

But the small woman was too strong for her. With her knees she pinned Jessica's shoulders and seized her head swiftly in hard brown hands.

The pain was sudden, sharp. Jessica shrieked. Peri swore. A severe wrench. Another pain.

"Jack!" she cried. But he was not there to hear her nor to stop the pain.

Then, it was done. Peri released her and sprang to her feet. "Stupid girl," she bellowed. "Stupid, stupid girl. It is a miracle I did not pierce your skull instead of your miserable ears. Komar is a fool!" And spitting on the ground, she stamped out of the tent.

Jessica felt tears burn her eyes. She turned over and punched at the rug under her head. The white cloth dropped from her neck, and she saw drops of blood on it. Furiously, she ripped it in two and flung the pieces against the tent flap. She tore the bangles from her arms and legs and threw them against the silver pitchers and bronze caskets, making these sound like ringing shields. Then she fell to her knees and screamed, "You bastards! All of you! Peri! Ashtar! Mother! Father!" And suddenly, she began to sob. Hot tears stained her fine new clothes, but, holding and rocking herself, still she wept. A decade's worth of weeping. "Why did I come here?" she cried.

And then through her tears, she saw Jack's face, haggard and gaunt. He pushed the hair away from his eyes with a gesture so familiar it hurt. She called his name, but he disappeared. And in his place were Gabdon's soft eyes. She remembered the muscled back beneath her and the silky mane under her hand; she felt the ground tilt, the wind course past her. And suddenly she was strong and full. The flames of her fury and of her pain sank into ashes, and when the ashes too slid away, they left a golden core that throbbed and shone in her breast. "The malat," she murmured. And then: "Horsemaster."

A sharp prick startled her, and the glow faded. She looked down. Her right hand was bleeding. She stared at the blood and remembered having said something. What was it, she wondered. Her eyes focused on the dagger she held in her bleeding hand. She did not recall picking it up. On the dagger's chased silver hilt was the design of a horse's head surrounded by stars. Her hand twinged. She shook herself. "Look in the corner by that big casket. There is a blue pot." It was Noura, but her voice, the points of light, seemed fainter.

Jessica glanced around the tent and found the pot.

"Open it. Put the ointment on your hand and earlobes. It will ease the sting."

Jessica dipped her left index finger into the thick cream and awkwardly smoothed it on to her right palm and then her earlobes. Noura was right. It helped the pain at once.

"Noura, where did this dagger come from," Jessica asked.

But Noura did not answer.

"Please tell me."

But Noura could—or would—not.

"Noura, are you all right?"

"I . . . am . . . well," Noura answered haltingly. "Tend . . . to . . . your . . . hand."

Jessica nodded. She replaced the blue pot. Then, quickly binding a strip of the bloodied, rent, white cloth around her hand, she began to scrabble around in the caskets. Soon she found a leather scabbard that perfectly fit the dagger's blade.

She thrust the sheathed dagger into her girdle and then began to gather and don the bangles she had flung away. When she was finished, she poured and drank a single cup of wine and dashed the cup to the floor.

"With Gabdon's help, I will find you, Jack. Even if I have to kill the rest of them. Even if, when I see him again, I have to kill Ashtar. Especially Ashtar."

And, head erect despite the heavy earrings, she strode out of the tent.

# 25

THE TREES had wispy, feathery leaves. She stood beneath them for a long while until she grew tired. Then she returned to her tent and amused herself by examining the treasures there. For the rest of the day, Komar and Peri left her alone. They were giving her time to recover from the indignity of the ear piercing. She had overheard Peri in the neighboring tent complaining about the time she was costing them, but, oddly enough, Komar defended her.

"The girl is frightened and alone. Let her be. She will not be a hindrance," he said. "And you know as well as I that soon we will need another partner. You cannot very well slip through narrow windows with a belly like a shoni melon."

Jessica was surprised by the tenderness in his voice. He had held a knife to *her* belly and she could not think of him as gentle to anyone. Peri's reply surprised her as well.

"We have waited so long for this child. Bodar grant that it be born sound and whole. Else you will have good reason to leave me." The woman sounded on the verge of tears.

"My wife, I will never leave you. Even if you bear me no children for the rest of our days. I do not believe in the custom of abandoning a barren mate. And I am not so certain that I believe in Bodar either . . ."

"Hush, for Golgon's sake!" Then loudly, Peri proclaimed, "Do not heed him, O Bodar! He has dwelt under the sun too long and needs your gentle light to bring back his wits."

Komar laughed. "You would have been happier as a priestess than as a thief. Perhaps it is *you* who should abandon *me*."

"Never," Peri said fiercely. Then she let out a small cry.

Jessica heard Komar ask in an agitated voice, "What is wrong?"

"Nothing," Peri answered quickly. "It is nothing. Better see to it that that foolish girl does not run away."

"Run away? To where could she run? I will let her be while you and I rest."

Then they were silent. Jessica tried to blot out what she had just heard. She did not want to feel any sympathy for these people. But she could not erase the small circle of compassion that formed near her heart.

LATER in the day, Komar came into the tent where Jessica lay resting on a pile of rugs. He carried a cup. "Drink," he said. "It will help you awake."

She took it, wondering why Peri had not brought it to her as she had the other food and drink, and sniffed the contents.

"There is no poison in it, I assure you," he said wryly. "I have just given some to Peri to wake her. She too is tired this day."

Gingerly, she took a sip. "Coffee!" she exclaimed.

He laughed outright. "What did you expect?"

"It's just . . . I haven't had any since . . ." She faltered and fell silent.

He looked curiously at her. "The earrings are very becoming.

But it is strange that a Dakara girl should not have pierced ears," he said softly. The irony in his voice did not escape her.

*He suspects something,* she thought. *But what? That I'm not from Dakara. So what? He can't know I'm really from Wisconsin. That it's . . .* She went cold. *I don't know where I am or when I am. How long have I been gone?* An image of her mother came to her—her mother standing by the door, her hair uncombed, eyes bloodshot. Her usually carefully groomed mother in an unpressed dirty dress. Waiting. For the police. The phone. The neighbors. For any sign from her daughter, who was so far away. And an unfamiliar ache filled Jessica. Then the image faded and the pain was gone. She shook herself. No, she thought, my mother doesn't feel that way. But the shadow of the ache remained. And to her chagrin, she found she had spilled the coffee and was clutching Komar's hand. She let him go at once and braced herself for more abuse.

But he merely righted the fallen cup and said quietly, "Perhaps one day you will see your home again."

She felt the tears spring to her eyes.

"I know what it is like to be far from home. My parents, I have not seen them in many a year."

She nodded, lowering her eyes so he could not see them.

"There are those who wish to capture Peri and myself. That is why . . . I do not wish to harm you, Vashti. Trust me."

*Trust. I wish I could trust someone,* she thought. The press of the hard leather scabbard against her side stopped the tears from flowing. "How can I trust a thief like you?" she said harshly.

He recoiled as if she'd slapped him and said coldly, "If you desire more coffee, you may get it yourself. We leave when the sun touches the horizon." Then he turned and was gone.

# 26

OBLIVIOUS TO the setting sun, the last of the heat, the sizable human burden it carried, the camel plodded steadily, its single hump rolling like some queer pile of hay on a wagon. Occasionally, it let out a wide-mouthed cry—a cross between a lion's roar and a bull sea lion's bellow.

"Shut up, you old harridan," Komar would chide, but not without amusement. Then, he would whistle his curious little tune.

Perched atop the big animal's shaggy hump and leaning hard against Komar's chest and strong arms holding the reins, Jessica bumped and swayed with each step. The desert was silent. She began to think about the tapestry strapped to Moofta's back. Komar had said something about selling the donkeys in Medwar. She would have to transfer the tapestry to the camel, and that would be no mean feat. *Unless I make up some kind of story about the donkey being a pet. But I doubt . . .*

"You smell like a dusk rose, little Vashti. Bahsboosa will be pleased indeed," Komar said, interrupting her thoughts.

Jessica's mouth tightened.

"You will make this easier for all of us if you will trust me," Komar said in a kinder voice.

"Have you sent out your spies?" she responded gruffly.

He snorted. "Ah, little Vashti. Let us stick to business, eh?" he said in his usual sardonic manner. "Well, do not worry. Do your job well, and you will have your answer soon enough. Soon enough."

She was about to reply, when a shrill cry from Peri made

them both start. "Look behind! Look behind!" she yelled.

Komar wheeled the camel, and he and Jessica saw in the distance, under the blue haze of twilight, a cloud of dust.

"Horses," he said.

"Raiders," Peri rasped.

"No, I do not think so. There were no reports of raiders. At any rate, there is nothing to do, nowhere to escape. We will ride on at the same pace and let them overtake us."

It was not long before the cloud of dust swelled and the horses appeared, bearing heavily armed men. They soon surrounded the little caravan.

"Halt," the leader commanded, pulling alongside Komar and Jessica. "Where are you going?"

"Medwar," Komar answered calmly. "Delivering goods to Bahsboosa, the merchant."

The soldier laughed and tugged at Jessica's scarf. "This the goods?" he asked.

Komar laughed. "I see you too know Bahsboosa."

Jessica indignantly pushed away the soldier's hand.

"A temper," he said, and he laughed again.

"And you, where do you go?" Komar asked, casually.

"To join Shadoor Smerdis's army. They say a glorious battle begins within a fortnight, to secure the throne for our land."

"Luck to you then and to the friends of Smerdis."

The soldier saluted with his sword.

"Wealth to you from the merchant Bahsboosa," he answered and grinned. Then he rode to the head of the troop and called, "Ho do kai."

The horsemen filed neatly behind him, and glowing like fox-fire, they soon disappeared over the steadily darkening desert.

Komar watched them go. Then he spat on the ground. "May he rot in Zaboon," he growled and, spurring the camel, led his caravan to Medwar village.

# 27

THE JAGGED desert brush gave way to trees rising wraith-like in the moonlight. Jessica could make out graceful fronds and, once, a great hanging cluster of fruit. Presently, the sand seemed smoother, and the camel rocked and jerked less. Then the first houses appeared, gray and silent as the stone from which they were built.

More houses, a few glowing yellow-orange from the fires burning inside. Then, a party of men, their bearded faces sweating in the torchlight, staggered near them. One pressed the torch close to Jessica and in a belch of foul breath said, "So, who's thish pretty? For me. A danshing girl for Mutma?"

"How about a little danshe?" another slurred, trying to pull her from the camel.

But Komar commanded, "Out of my way, you besotted fools!" and spurred the camel ahead, leaving Peri to rail at the drunken men from her donkey.

At the end of what seemed to be a densely populated street stood a house larger than the others and studded here and there with bits of glass that winked in the moonlight.

"Say nothing and watch carefully," Komar said, dismounting.

Jessica nodded and let him help her down. Her legs, stiff from the camel's huge girth, buckled, and she had to be propped up by Peri's rough hands and donkey switch.

Komar strode to the wooden door and knocked hard.

In answer, a small light appeared near a grated, oblong window.

"Who's there?" said a high-pitched voice.

"Radba," Komar replied tersely.

A pause, and then, "Have you brought the merchandise?"

"Yes."

"One moment."

The light disappeared. Jessica felt her legs fumble and the thrust of Peri's switch in the small of her back.

Then the door was thrown open and an immensely fat gentleman holding a taper waddled out. "Well, well, Radba. It has been a long time," he said, in his absurd voice.

The effect was of a piccolo in the body of a tuba. Jessica had to bite her knuckles to stop herself from laughing.

"A long time, Bahsboosa," Komar agreed.

"And your woman," he inclined his jowled head toward Peri. "How is she? With child yet?"

Jessica waited for Peri to snap, "*She* is quite well." But to her amazement, Peri began to giggle and scrape, and nod.

"Ah, Bodar be praised. May your babe be healthy and fat," said Bahsboosa. He said nothing at all to Jessica, nor did he look at her. "Well, come in, come in. Tea is almost ready. I would offer you some little cakes, but I am afraid that fool baker ran out." And maneuvering his fleshy form with difficulty, he ushered them into his house.

After he lit several large tapers in their scrolled iron stands, all the while chatting about the excessive cost of candles these days, he pointed to several threadbare pillows and urged them to sit. As Jessica bent to do so, she felt Peri's hand prod her erect. She had no choice but to stand awkwardly behind the merchant.

"So, you avoided the sand storm?" he asked.

"No, it avoided us," Komar replied.

The fat man laughed. "Did you meet with anything of interest on your journey?"

"We did speak with some soldiers who said they were off to join Smerdis's army. They spoke of a battle soon to occur."

"Ah," said the merchant, "there is so much talk. I expect there will be a war, but it cannot affect the likes of us, can it, Radba?" His thick lips parted in a complacent smile.

"I much doubt it."

"One shadoor is as good as another, eh?" He laughed.

"True. As long as he does not affect business."

Bahsboosa's face lost its complacency. "Yes," he said. There was a pause, and then he smiled once again, said, "Well, let us have tea," and reached for a tiny silver bell with a soft, well-groomed hand.

*They act as if I don't exist,* Jessica thought. *In one minute I'll run out of here. Go to the nearest house and . . . And do what? What? There is nothing I can do. Now . . . yet.*

Her thoughts were interrupted by a stooped and wizened servant woman whose wrinkled hands shook as she carried the tea things.

"Ah, here is the tea," Bahsboosa said smoothly.

But as the servant bent to lay down the tray, an acute palsy seemed to seize her, and she spilled several large drops on the merchant's massive thigh.

"Clumsy oaf," he screamed, cuffing her head. "Watch what you are about!"

The servant immediately began to apologize profusely in a cracked and nasal voice. There was something oddly familiar about that servant, Jessica thought. But before she could figure out what it was, Bahsboosa, in a storm of imprecations, sent the old woman scurrying from the room.

When the servant was gone, the merchant quickly recovered his equanimity and poured tea for everyone but Jessica.

After what seemed hours of polite talk and tea drinking, Bahsboosa put down his cup and said, "And now, Radba, I believe you have something to show me."

Komar nodded and motioned to Peri, who arose and led Jessica to Bahsboosa. The merchant took Jessica's hand. She shuddered at the touch.

"Ah, she is yet shy," he said, with great delight. "Come into the light, my dear, so that I may see you." He drew her into a circle of brightness and, with such delicacy, as though he were unwrapping the silver foil from an exceptional piece of chocolate, took off her turban and scarf.

"Lovely!" he exclaimed. "Perfect!" Then he asked, "My child, what is your name?"

"Vashti," she answered quietly.

"Vashti, can you dance the somora and the pirtu?"

"Yes," she lied, not knowing what on earth he was talking about. Then, impishly, she added, "And the polka."

Komar coughed. Peri glared at her. And the merchant asked, "The polka? What is the polka?"

"A dance from Dakara," Jessica said.

"Ah," said Bahsboosa, as if that explained everything. "Well, I hope to see you dance at the palace of the Emir Fatoosh."

Jessica bowed gracefully.

"And most especially the polka."

Komar coughed again, this time so hard that Bahsboosa had to ask him if he needed more tea. He breathed an audible sigh of relief when Komar politely declined.

Jessica remained standing as Komar and Bahsboosa haggled over her price and as Bahsboosa triumphantly paid two pijars less than Komar originally demanded. And she remained standing throughout the extensive farewells, the entreaties to return soon, the bundling off of Komar and Peri on their respective mounts.

When they were gone, Bahsboosa rumbled into another room and returned with a mound of tasselled and embroidered pillows. Dropping them on the threadbare ones and sinking onto them, he sighed and said, coaxingly, "How pretty you look in the waning candlelight. Would you dance for me? Old Bahsboosa would so like to see you dance."

Warily, she shook her head.

He hoisted himself on one elbow. "No? Not one little dance? Not one little dance for an old man who has not long to see pretty girls dance?"

Again, she shook her head.

He hauled his bulk up and advanced upon her, blotting out the amber candlelight. "Come, come, girl. I paid good money for you."

Her hand reaching for the sheathed blade hidden at her waist, she said in as faltering a voice as she could manage, "Please sir, I am very tired."

"Tired! A dancing girl tired?" he began, but a commotion made him stop.

It was the old servant, who had crept in silently "so as not to disturb the master," she said, but who had dropped the pot while gathering the tea things.

"Imbecile," the merchant bellowed. "You will pay for that pot out of your wages. And then you will leave this house. I must have been drugged when I took on such an old fool!"

The servant burst into tears and fled. Again Jessica wondered at what seemed familiar. Then Bahsboosa rolled back to her and passed a hand over his face, which seemed suddenly to sag under its weighty load. He yawned hugely.

"Weary . . ." he said. "So sleepy . . . Now . . . you . . . go to your room. There . . . on the right . . . Must go to sleep." He staggered to his room, yawning and muttering to himself.

Jessica smiled exultantly to herself and walked swiftly to her room.

# 28

IT IS a contest of wills, and I am losing. It grows hard to speak. I do not wish to tell the Messenger. She must not grow fearful. She must not fail. Fear fills me, pushes up in my throat. The demons are loosed in my skull. Terrors innumerable. And madness all around. And over and over beats the drum: worthless, worthless, worthless. Noura is nothing, nothing, nothing. If I let go, it will leave me in peace. I hold on still, but my grasp grows weaker, and I long to sink into blissful oblivion, to be the nothing the voice tells me I am.

Sheets of fire. Double-headed snakes. Wind of ice. The Doomor. The Doomor. The Doomor. Bodar, Kadi, Golgon. Spitting spite. Crush the . . . bat-headed . . . O merciful gods . . . Help me . . . I cannot . . . The Messenger . . . O Gods, I see her

... face ... her .. .face .. I cannot be ... cannot ... This is a trick ... Crueler than all the others ... Lies ... Lies ... Double-headed snakes ... O Gods!

# 29

ILLUMINATED BY a small taper undoubtedly lit by the frazzled servant, Jessica's "room" consisted of several worn rugs thrown over a pallet of straw, a wooden table that had once been a brightly painted treasure, but was now faded and so relegated to guests, and a fragment of a mirror. But the most important aspect of the room was its window. The only accessible ungrated window in Bahsboosa's house, Komar had said.

"Why?" Jessica had asked.

"Probably because he is too miserly to grate it; after all, it is only for guests," Komar told her.

The silk was to be carried bolt by bolt from the adjoining storeroom and handed out of the window to Komar, who would be waiting below. His funny obligato would be the signal.

Jessica sat down, grateful for the straw. *What if we are caught*, she wondered. *Do they put you in prison in this place? Or maybe they do things like cutting off a thief's right hand.*

"I'm scared. I'm so scared," she said quietly. "Oh, Gabdon if only you could help me. If only I could help you."

Suddenly, she felt such a burst of love for the horse that her hands flew to her heart. She wanted to stroke his soft muzzle and look once more into those deep, quiet eyes.

And then, she became angry. "What's *wrong* with me? Why the hell am I thinking of that damn horse? He caused all this trouble in the first place. The precious son of a god. What a crock!"

She heard a horse's snuffle, and before she could stop herself, she cried out, "Gabdon!" and rushed to the window. Only then did she hear the snatch of a tune, and a voice that whispered, "Keep your head and be quiet."

It was Komar, astride a dark horse. Peri too was on horseback. Jessica's disappointment was so bitter that she moaned.

"Pleased to see me, I presume," Komar said mordantly. "The drug has worked?"

"Yes," she answered.

"Good. Then go to the storeroom and fetch the silk."

Her whole body jangling, Jessica grasped the small candle from the table and passed into the hallway and down the short corridor. The storeroom to which Komar had directed her, like the other rooms of the house, was sealed only by a heavy curtain. She drew it aside and entered. By the feeble light of the candle, what she saw startled her even more than the riches in Komar's tent. There were no caskets nor piles of jewels. No jugs or mirrors. But every conceivable type of fabric lay in neat piles that rose to the high ceiling. She could see raw wool, spun wool, huge rugs of glistening fur, brocades of such gold and silver only a king would dare wear them. And silk. Silk in shades she thought only peacocks and tulips possessed. She seized a bolt of royal purple and cautiously pulled back the curtain.

At the entrance to her room, she thought she heard a thump behind her. She whirled around, but saw nothing.

Komar was still beneath the window. "Excellent, little Vashti," he said when he saw the silk. He reached up for it, but Jessica held it fast.

"First," she said, "your promise."

"Do not tell her. First get the silk," snapped Peri.

"Peri is so trusting," Komar said. Then he grew sober. "We have no time to argue. I will tell you. There is no stranger come to the Imperial Palace. But there is an odd story concerning Gamesh, the blacksmith's son. It seems he is not dead after all."

At the name Gamesh, Jessica nearly dropped the silk.

"Daughter of an assassin, watch out!" Peri hissed.

Supporting herself and the silk against the ledge, Jessica asked, "What of Gamesh?"

"It seems he was captured on the way to warn Tarkesh of the impending war. He is to be the gift at the Horse Sacrifice." He paused, trying to search Jessica's face framed by the dark window, but could see nothing.

"Go on," she insisted, the pulse in her temple throbbing wildly.

"The boy insists he is not Gamesh. He says his name is Jack. He says he . . ."

But Jessica did not hear the rest. She lurched and fell from the window onto Komar's frightened horse, which shied as Komar struggled with the reins.

"The silk!" screamed Peri, clutching her belly.

"Must save Jack," Jessica said between labored breaths. "Never . . . mind . . . silk."

"Yes," said the high-pitched voice at the window where Jessica had been a moment before. "Never mind the silk."

"Flee, Peri, flee," Komar bellowed, desperately spurring his horse as a crowd of men holding great clubs suddenly filled the small street and began to close in.

The last thing Jessica remembered before the heavy wood struck her forehead was the face of the old servant standing in the window next to Bahsboosa. And in that instant, she knew why it was familiar. It was Ashtar's face.

# 30

SHE REMEMBERED little of the journey except for the painful jogging of the cart in which she lay bound hand and foot.

Sometimes her head would throb viciously, but somehow she could never reach it, never touch the source of the pain.

Sometimes, the jogging would stop, a coarse hand would trickle something warm and sweet into her dry mouth, and the pain would ease. But not for long. Never for long.

When the cart reached its destination, she scarcely felt the rough arms lift her down and toss her on an icy stone floor. She wanted only to sleep. A sleep without dreams.

But dreams came. The first was pleasant: a memory of a golden spring day when she and Jack climbed a small hill to fly the magnificent kite he had made. It was a winged man, an Icarus. She pointed the story out to Jack in her fairy tale book. He was captured by the tale of the young man whose wax wings melted when he flew too near the sun, causing him to plummet to earth. "I'll make a man whose wings won't melt," Jack said. And he did, though the kite never got anywhere near the sun. But it flew high, a frail, pale shape against the intense blue of the sky. Jack ran, ran, ran with the kite, his dark hair flopping into his eyes. *He's going to take off and soar*, Jessica thought, and she wanted to fly with him. The dream ended abruptly, the way a film breaks in a projector.

The second dream was brief and strange. It began just as Jessica's dreams used to begin—with the horse clopping slowly toward her. She held out her hand. The horse stood still, his head slightly cocked, as though listening. Then, a rich, eloquent, disembodied voice announced, "Behold Gabdon, Maker of Masters, Unmaker of Masters, Son of Kadi, Horse God of Sharoon. Ma-lat-El-Ma-lat. Power of the Power. Essence of the Essence." Gabdon neighed and bared his teeth in a big, horsey grin.

And Jessica began to laugh. "Oh, you big, silly animal, you," she said, shocking herself a little. "Come here and let me give you a hug."

With a snort, Gabdon trotted over and put his nose in her palm. She wrapped her arms around his neck. "What do they want of you? Horse God's son! Why can't they let you run in a field and eat oats." Gabdon gave a gentle whinny and nibbled

Jessica's ear. She laughed again. "You big lummox, you're tickling me." And she kissed his nose.

The dream ended abruptly. The third dream was not so pleasant. Jessica's mother was standing against a wall. Tears ran down her cheeks. Her hands were open, palms up, imploring. Jessica's father stood with his back to her mother, his arms outstretched to embrace Jessica. She ran to him, and as she reached his arms, he stepped away and she fell. When she got up, he was gone. Jessica walked over to her mother. She walked around her, poking, prodding with the horse-hilted dagger. Her mother did not bleed, nor cry out, nor even move. She just stood there in the same posture. Jessica picked up a plate laden with pancakes and smashed it over her mother's head. Still she didn't move. Then Jessica sank to her knees in front of her mother and began to cry. It was to no avail. Her mother did not budge. Finally, Jessica began to scream. She writhed and beat the floor. She kicked her feet, arched her body like an infant. Great bellows erupted from her until, at last, she was exhausted. Then she fell into the black, dreamless sleep she'd prayed for.

How long she slept, she didn't know, but one morning, torn unwillingly from her slumber, she awoke to find herself staring into a face so begrimed and bruised she did not recognize it. A fetid smell assaulted her nostrils, and she retched violently.

"Daughter of misfortune, so you are finally awake," the face said.

Jessica coughed, swallowed several times, and finally, in a hoarse voice, said, "Where am I?"

"Where are you, child of misery? Za-ka, you are in the house of death."

"I don't understand."

"The Emir Fatoosh's dungeon, you fool," she spat. "To be tried, convicted and killed for robbing one of his merchants."

Then, to Jessica's horror, she realized that this creature was Peri. And she remembered it all: Komar, the fat merchant, the silk, the men with clubs and the servant with Ashtar's face. And Jack. And, lastly, Gabdon. Where was the tapestry now? Lost?

"Oh no, no," she rasped, and tried to raise herself.

"Lie down, idiot child, you are not strong enough," Peri said, grasping her arm.

"Must . . . Jack . . ." Jessica began, but her throat went dry and she gagged.

"That is the talk that lost us the silk—and now our lives," Peri hissed.

The gagging left Jessica weak, and for a long time she said nothing. Then she asked, "Your child? Is it well?"

Peri touched her belly. "It lives."

"And the donkeys? What happened to the donkeys?"

Peri looked at her as though she had lost her mind. "They're probably in the stable until after our trial. Then the emir can 'officially' appropriate them."

"Is there a way out? To the stable?"

"Out of here, you simpleton? Have you never heard of Fatoosh's sanctuary? That is the nickname they give this prison. Everyone who enters is safe, safe from ever leaving again."

"There must be a way." She paused, and felt in her girdle for the dagger. It was gone. Fighting panic, she pushed her fist hard against her palm. "There must be a way," she repeated, "Komar . . ."

Peri turned her head so that Jessica could not see her trembling lips. "Komar is . . ."

"Dead?" whispered Jessica.

"Yes."

"Oh no," Jessica keened softly. "No."

"I tell you yes. And you are the cause!"

And Jessica began to weep without quite knowing why.

THE TRIAL was mercifully brief. Bahsboosa testified that this woman, and here he pointed at Peri, standing in a circle of stone benches on which the emir's council sat in formidably white robes, brought him a *servant*. (Dancing girls were expressly forbidden for sale according to Shadoor Tarkesh's laws, which were still upheld in theory, although the emir himself bought dancing girls and although the Shadoor was virtually deposed in the minds of many of his subjects.) The servant had been sold for the express purpose of stealing his silk. He described how he tasted the drug in his tea, feigned sleep and followed this girl—here motioning at Jessica standing next to Peri—from his storeroom, where she took a bolt of silk to her room and pitched it from the window to Radba, the thief (recently slain), waiting below. The man who had struck Jessica confirmed the remainder of the story.

Peri was asked if she had anything to say, and she uttered a curse so violent the guards dragged her from the room.

Jessica's turn. There was much she could say: I was captured in the desert by Komar and Peri; deserted by my "friend" Ashtar; caught in a sandstorm; I am not from this land; spare me; I have been wronged. She had meant to say these things, meant to stand there in her now-ragged finery and plead for her life as eloquently as she could.

But instead, she meekly bowed her head and, in a low voice, said, "We are very poor. Have mercy on us."

"There is no mercy for thieves," the chief councilman said coldly. Then he ordered the guards, "Take her back to the cell; we will confer now about how justice shall be meted."

Jessica was not surprised when, an hour later, a young guard with a girlish face entered the cell and announced, "The council has judged you, Peri of Somor, and you, Vashti of Dakara, to be guilty of thievery. The sentence is death. Peri of Somor, you will be hanged in the Paltar Square tomorrow at sunrise. Vashti of Dakara, the council has decreed death by hanging for you as well . . ."

He paused, and she let out a long sigh.

"However," the guard continued, "the merchant Bahsboosa has interceded on your behalf, citing your youth and innocence, and has requested the council to indenture you to him as his servant for the remainder of his life."

A rush of breath, a sharp sound from Jessica's throat, while Peri swore at this turn of events, this release from death of the cause of all her misfortune.

The guard's voice lowered. "I am sorry," he began in a rush.

"You are young . . . It is hard . . . Here, some water."

But Jessica scarcely heard him. *Indentured to that fat man with eyes like black grapes and the too-soft hands. Not that, no. Better to die. Better to—* But she stopped suddenly and drew herself up straight. In a dry, clear voice she asked the guard, "Tell me. The Horse Sacrifice. Has it been?"

The guard looked puzzled at the question and did not answer at once. Then he said, "No, it . . . has not been." Then he fell silent.

Jessica caught her breath. "Tell me one more thing. As Bahsboosa's servant, may I request he let me retain my faithful old donkey Moofta to take on my errands?"

"It has already been sold," the guard said.

"Oh no . . . I mean . . . is Moofta already gone?"

"No, I do not think so."

"Then, I beg permission to bid him goodbye. In the name of Gabdon." Her hand flew to her mouth. *Why did I say that?* she thought. *Why?*

The guard regarded her strangely. Then he said, "I have no more time for talk. You must prepare for your departure after the hanging." Then he left rapidly, bolting the iron-studded door behind him.

"I'm so stupid. Stupid! I must get out. Ask Bahsboosa. It's possible Jack is still alive. Ashtar said the Red Lady would not kill him. But Ashtar is a liar and a bastard. Oh God! Oh God!" Jessica muttered, running her hands frantically through her disheveled hair. Then she turned to meet Peri's intense gaze, a mixture of malevolence and awe.

"Vashti of Dakara," the dark woman said. "I do not think you come from Dakara at all. And by Golgon, I do not know who or what you are. But if you can summon Gabdon, bid him to save my child. Save my child!" And, wailing "Save my child!" over and over, Peri hurled herself at Jessica's feet.

# 31

JESSICA SIPPED at the pungent water the guard had left in the cell and regarded Peri with pity. Stripped of her surliness, the small woman sat hunched and grief-stricken in a corner. "I do not want my child to die," she muttered. "I do not want my child to die."

"Peri, I have heard much of Gabdon in . . . in . . . Dakara. I wish he could help us. But I cannot summon him," Jessica said gently. It really was not a lie. Without the tapestry, she could not summon him.

Wiping her eyes and nose with her sleeve, Peri said in something of her old manner, "Then you are a foolish dreamer. No one can find Gabdon save he who can summon him."

"I'm sorry I can't do anything," Jessica said.

"Sorrow will not save my child," Peri said bitterly.

"No, it won't," Jessica agreed quietly. "But still I am sorry."

Peri grunted and turned her face to the wall.

Forming, discarding, reforming plans to escape from Bahsboosa when he came to claim her, Jessica sat silently, watching, waiting for the guards to appear to take Peri and then herself to their respective destinies. Once I wanted to kill her, she thought, staring in the darkness at the dim outline that was Peri. To plunge a dagger into her wretched heart. But no more. I would save her if I could. But it's no use. I don't even know if I can save myself.

In her sleep, Peri moaned and cried out, "Komar!"

Jessica shambled over to her. "Hush," she said, stroking the woman's hot brow. "It was a dream."

What time was it? How long was this night? There were no windows to let in the moon's silver or the sun's gold.

For many hours, Jessica had cursed Ashtar with every breath she drew for leading her—and Jack, Komar, Peri, all of them—to this end. Now, drained of her anger, she sat with her eyes closed against the darkness. Beneath her futile, caressing hands, Peri stirred fitfully. "Horsemaster, O Horsemaster, save me!"

"Hush," Jessica said again, opening her eyes. Something danced before them. Pinpricks of light, like tiny sacred flames in an unholy cave.

"Noura," she said. "Are you here?"

The light grew stronger. Shafts of silver pierced the blackness.

"Noura!"

The room filled with white light. Jessica felt herself lifted, suspended, as though she were sitting on a cloud and could see all that transpired below, but could not reach, could not touch any of it. *I am dreaming*, Jessica said. But it did not feel like a dream. She heard the muttering first and knew that someone was being tormented. Red-tongued mouths, foul-breathed, shrieking and hissing. Words she could not understand. But she knew their import. Fear. Fear so palpable it sat on her chest like stone. Yet it did not crush her, for it was not she they were meant to crush.

"Help me, Messenger, help me," a voice cried above the din. It was then Jessica saw the misty figure, holding its arms out to her. "Help me!" Noura cried. "Messenger, help me!"

Jessica tried to lift her arms, but she could not. "Noura, I am here. How can I help?" she tried to say. But her words fell darkly and did not reach the princess.

Then Noura screamed and shrank to the ground. The scene came into sharp focus. The Red Lady appeared, smiling, extravagant with power. She clapped her hands. The picture seemed to break apart and reassemble.

Darkness. Cold gray. Another figure. On a bench. Head in hands. "Help me. Help me, Jessica."

"Jack!" she called. "Jack!"

He picked up his head. The skin on his face looked translucent, pulled taut over his bones. "The tapestry. Give her the tapestry. She wants the tapestry," he said dully.

Once before she had been in a position to exchange the tapestry for her friend. But not now. "I would if I could. But I don't have it!" she cried.

"You will get it. She will find a way."

"How? What is the way? I'll do anything. I'll give her anything to free you," Jessica cried.

"No!" The word flashed, seared her eyes. "No. Do not. I beg of you!" Noura shouted, then screamed in pain as the mouths jabbered on.

The image of Jack disappeared. "Oh God, not again," Jessica wailed. Like a jigsaw puzzle, bits of light shifted once again and came together.

It was the tapestry she saw first, lit by the light of a golden throne. Then the Red Lady appeared, laughing, as a young man entered, crowned and dressed in purple, surrounded by grinning, gore-clotted guards. The Lady held out her hands. They were as red-smeared as the tip of Smerdis's sword. He clasped her hands and roared with laughter. Then he clapped, and two slaves came forward with something on a silver platter, something bearded and reeking of blood, an obscene dish for a new king.

"Oh my God!" Jessica screamed and retched. She shut her eyes, but the white light pierced the lids, and she was forced to open them.

The loathsome thing was gone. Now the Red Lady stood gripping Noura, whose back was to Jessica. "You fool, you fool," she said. "Show her your thoughts, will you? You will never be able to speak with her again." She shook Noura. The princess's hands grabbed at the air. Then the Red Lady spun her around. And for a moment, her agonized eyes met Jessica's so that for the first time Jessica saw Noura's face. It was the same as her own. "Oh my God," Jessica gasped, "It's me. Noura is me!" Noura opened her mouth once in a silent scream. Then she and the Red Lady were gone. And Jessica, arms wrapped around herself, keened into the darkness in the cold stone prison cell.

\*   \*   \*

SHE DID NOT move. She had not moved for hours. *How could we be the same? How? If we are one, why am I here?* But she knew the answer: Noura had failed at being the Messenger. Ashtar had said as much. But Noura still had to be Messenger, a "later" Noura. *Me. Me. Me. Me. Oh God, who the hell am I?* "I'm Jessica Walken, age fourteen, from Brown Deer, Wisconsin," she said aloud. "I'm in the ninth grade. My hobbies are . . . I don't have any hobbies." A sob escaped her. *If Noura dies, what happens to me? If I die . . . No. No! Keep thinking about Jessica. Jessica.* "Jessica has no pets, but she'd like a dog. Her best friend is Jack Manning . . . I can't. This isn't happening. It's all a dream. A bad dream . . . Jack is home. I'll see him when I wake up."

Footsteps outside the door, and the rattle of keys and bolts being drawn. Peri sat up with a gasp. "Golgon have mercy. Bodar have mercy. Kadi have mercy. Tecti have mercy," she chanted rapidly, pantingly.

Jessica went rigid once again.

The door groaned open and the young guard, bearing a torch, stepped inside.

Peri's voice rose frantically, "Kadi have mercy. Golgon have mercy . . ."

"Silence, woman," the guard commanded, and then announced, "His most illustrious Emir Fatoosh."

At once, Peri stopped gibbering. Jessica remained still.

Then, lit by torchlight and flanked by a dozen guards, into the dank, fetid cell stepped a tall, round-shouldered man with a long, rather vacant face. He motioned to three of the closest guards and they surrounded Jessica, shining their torches full upon her face.

"Well," said the emir, waggling his finger as he approached, "well, you have been a silly girl, have you not?"

Jessica began to giggle.

"Humph," said the emir. "You may laugh, but I assure you, your mother does not find your conduct at all humorous."

At this, Jessica laughed harder. Several of the guards began to snicker, and even the emir had to control a twitch in his upper lip.

"Uh-humph," he cleared his throat. "Well, let us get you out of here and fed and into some decent clothes and then we will depart, all right?"

Play with them, she thought. Remember it's just a bad dream. She hiccoughed. "All . . . right . . . hiccough . . . but where . . . hiccough . . . are . . . hiccough . . . we going?"

"Ah, what a sense of humor. Just like her mother," Emir Fatoosh answered. "You know perfectly well where we are going, so you can cease playing the jokes."

"I . . . hiccough . . . do?"

"You certainly do. Now, please allow me to escort you to my palace, Princess Noura," said the emir, extending his arm.

Jessica froze. Oh God, the nightmare was real.

"Princess Noura!" gasped Peri.

Sister, Noura had called her. Time twins? She'd heard something about—

"Princess Noura, mercy, mercy," Peri shrilled.

"Shut up, woman," growled a guard and raised a hand to hit her.

Then everything seemed to come together. Jessica squared her shoulders. "Enough!" she commanded, her hiccoughs gone. "You will not strike my companion. Nor will you hang her."

"But, my lady, the council—"

"To Zaboon with the council. I am Princess Noura."

The guard looked helplessly at the emir.

"As the princess commands," the emir replied deferentially. Then he said, "Oh. Before I forget. I believe this is yours." He handed her a leather scabbard.

She pulled out the dagger and stared at the silver horse's head. "Thank you," she said, and then, "There is something else of mine I'd like returned."

"Ask, and it shall be done."

"The donkey I rode—I have grown rather attached to him."

"Ah, the donkey. Oh yes, we will find . . . er . . . fetch him right away," the emir stammered.

"You do have him, do you not? The guard said he was sold but not yet taken."

"Why yes, yes, of course." He waved his hand in dismissal,

but beads of sweat formed above his lip. "Shall we go now, princess?" He extended his arm once again.

She laid her hand on it. "One more thing, Fatoosh. Is Gamesh . . . Has the horse sacrifice—" She stopped, fearful of the answer.

"Not yet," he said gravely. "It awaits your return."

"Ah," she said.

"You were very wrong to try to prevent a holy act," the emir chided.

Jessica merely smiled. "And now, my friend and I would both like a bath," she said.

The emir inclined his head. "But of course," he said, and carefully led Jessica and Peri from the cell.

# 32

FATOOSH HAD lied. Moofta the ass was already with a merchant, on his way to the seaport town of Tazira, which was many miles away from Medwar. Jessica discovered this in the midst of her bath (a handmaiden, whose sister, a scullion, had witnessed the departure, told her). She rose, dripping and frantic, from the tub and ran to the door. The horrified handmaiden sank to her knees, begged her to clothe herself and then begged forgiveness for being the bearer of bad news.

Jessica shoved her aside, dressed hurriedly and raced down to the stable. The keeper told her it was true; the donkey was gone.

"Oh no, what am I going to do?" she sobbed.

The keeper was as upset as the handmaiden. "Oh, Most Radiant Majesty, do not distress yourself. See, the emir will give you your pick of any donkey in the city. Of any animal, in fact. He told me to tell you so."

"I do not want any other donkey . . . Oh no, oh no—" Then, abruptly she stopped crying and asked, "Keeper, was the donkey sold as is? I mean, is something left of my friend—reins, an old rug, anything?"

"Not that I know of," the keeper said, ready to jump back in case the princess should strike him for his words. "But I will look," he said hurriedly.

He disappeared and returned with the emir.

"Now, now, are you still troubling yourself about that flea-bitten beast?" the emir said.

Jessica was trembling, but she tightened herself. She was, after all, the princess. "Fatoosh," she said coldly, "I command you to send however many riders it takes to find that merchant and my donkey."

"But princess . . ." he protested.

"I *command* you."

The emir bowed. "As you wish."

But by the next evening, neither Moofta nor the merchant had been found, and the emir told Jessica they could no longer put off leaving for the Imperial City.

She was sitting with her head in her hands when Peri entered the room.

"I will find the ass," Peri said bluntly.

Jessica looked up and replied with equal bluntness, "The emir's men could not. How can you?"

"I have ways."

Jessica shook her head. "You have gone through enough. You will be better off at home."

"I have no home."

"I will give you one then."

"That is very generous of you, but first I will find the donkey," Peri said in a voice both gruff and humble.

"Why are you willing to do this?"

"I owe my child's life to you, and I will return the favor if I can."

"Oh no, you don't owe your child's life to me. I almost cost you and the child your lives, as I cost Komar's."

Peri ignored her. "I will find the donkey and bring it to you at the Imperial City. I have unfinished business there anyway."

"What kind of business?"

"Never mind. It is my business." Peri scowled.

"No. You forget. I am Princess Noura. Everything is my business."

Peri looked at her with hooded eyes. "Two people know the truth of that. You are one. I am the other."

"What do you mean?"

"A little matter of unpierced ears."

Jessica regarded her silently.

"I will ask no questions, neither about you nor about why you need that precious donkey so much. Just give me leave to bring it to you at the palace."

"But you're pregnant. You're not strong enough to travel."

Peri laughed. "What strange mother bore you? I have all the strength I need."

Jessica sighed and finally said, "Very well. I will tell them to watch for you."

"You will not regret it."

"I hope I won't."

Peri turned to go, but Jessica called her back. "Good luck, Peri. To all of us. If you find the ass, you will be doing more than you dream."

Peri nodded curtly and left.

Jessica was surprised to discover that they were to embark for the Imperial City in the daytime. But she said nothing lest she reveal an ignorance Princess Noura would not have. She had been bathed, fed and dressed in a simple, but finely made rose-colored robe over which she wore a long, bone-white coat. Then Fatoosh himself appeared to inform her that the palanquin was ready. She nodded, pretending to understand what he was talking about.

She had done a good job pretending so far, she thought. But it was not difficult. They all believed she was Noura anyway. But the Red Lady knew differently. She knew about Jessica.

She knew it all. *Why doesn't she just kill me,* Jessica asked herself. *Why doesn't she just seize the tapestry? Unless she doesn't know where it is? But that's impossible. She's a sorcerer. She knows everything. So what is she doing?*

Jessica didn't know the answer. And so, when she was alone, her hands shook and she could not control her lips. *I have to believe I can still rescue him,* she thought. *I have to, or I'll be better off dead.*

Fatoosh gestured toward the door, and she followed him out into the sunlight where four brawny men, their faces already beaded with sweat, held aloft a square box supported by two long, horizontal poles. The box was covered with brocade and fringes. Fatoosh parted the curtain to reveal the lustrous cushions inside. And then Jessica understood that she was to ride inside, to be borne, safe from the blistering sunlight, by these four slaves sweltering and stumbling through the sand on sore, calloused feet.

She realized that she could not say, "No, I won't ride in this." Noura would never act that way. And, at the same time, she felt the strong attractiveness of power—how exciting it was to command such obedience, how obvious that a princess should deserve such comfort. As she climbed into the palanquin, she felt she had ridden in such a manner many times before and had always taken it—and the four slaves—for granted. The thought sickened her then, and she shuddered and let her warm tears stain the silken cushions on which she sat all the way to the Imperial City.

A MULTITUDE of cheers and huzzahs. The tinkle of cymbals, the thrum of tambours. She wanted to pull aside the heavy brocade and look out at the streets, which had to be lined with people. She wanted to see the houses, the date-laden palms, the carved stone pillars she knew were there. But she could not.

The palanquin stopped. She felt the press of bodies gathered around it, jostling for a better view.

"Zaka, watch where you are going!" growled one of the bearers.

A sudden roar from the crowd. Then shouts of, "Look, look.

He comes!" "It is Smerdis, Talliya's son. Long live Smerdis!" and "Long live the shadoor!"

A hand parted the brocade curtain, and a burly young man in tunic and dress armor offered Jessica his arm.

"You look as if you do not recognize your own brother, Noura," he said.

Jessica stared hard at the squarish face with its thin lips and close-set eyes. "No, you are wrong, Smerdis," she replied. "I would know you anywhere. But why did you come yourself to fetch me?"

"Why should I not come to fetch you?" he said churlishly.

At once she understood. "Did the Red . . . er . . . did Mother suggest it?"

"Yes. She said it would please the crowd," he answered.

She smiled slightly. "And so it has." And she stepped down from the palanquin.

The sunlight dazzled. She blinked and shaded her eyes while the crowd cheered and threw small tributes of flowers, fruit and coins at her feet.

Smerdis put his mouth close to her ear. "Listen, we are circulating the story that you were ill and went to the Shabash Spa for a cure. No one must know you've been in prison." He wrinkled his nose at the word.

"Half of Medwar knows," she said.

Smerdis looked at her in exasperation. "We have paid the coffers of Medwar a fat sum to restore the Temple of Golgon there. Fatoosh will keep his people silent."

But Jessica wasn't listening. She was looking over Smerdis's shoulder at a bent and wizened figure threading its way toward the great stone palace. She broke away from Smerdis, wanting to run. "You there!" she shouted. "Stop!" But instantly, she realized that a princess would not act that way. "Guard!" she called to the brawny man nearest her. "Follow that person, and when you have caught him, bring him to me."

The guard obeyed at once. Jessica saw him run through the throng, roughly shoving people aside, to reach his quarry. He turned down an arched passageway, and Jessica, straining to stay put, lost sight of him.

"Let us go inside now," said Smerdis, who engrossed in smiling upon the crowd, had neither seen nor heard the exchange.

"No, I must wait," she said.

The crowd, delighted to have the princess in their midst for so long a time, stretched out their eager hands to touch her. The guards forced them back.

Smerdis was fuming at his sister. "What are you waiting for, you impossible, willful child?" he hissed into her ear, all the while smiling and waving at the still cheering crowd. "You had better not spoil my campaign."

Jessica kept her eyes fixed on the archway and said, "I asked a guard to bring to me a . . . friend."

Smerdis grunted his disapproval and then began an impromptu and confused speech of welcome to the crowd. Jessica did not listen to it.

When the guard returned, he was pale, panting and alone. He knelt before Jessica. "Princess, I have failed. The man you bade me fetch v-vanished. Into the air. I a-await your p-punishment."

Jessica closed her eyes a moment. Then she opened them and said, "You have done your best."

"Thank you for forgiving your wretched servant," the guard said.

Smerdis, who this time had heard, said, "You let him off too lightly. You will never make much of a ruler."

*Thank God for that, thought Jessica.*

"May we now go inside, Sister?" asked Smerdis sarcastically. "Mother has a few things to say to you."

She nodded, and he gave a signal. Ten men strained at the great wooden doors of the palace until, at last, they opened with an enormous groan.

Jessica took a deep breath. *I'm coming, Jack, I'm coming,* she said silently. And then, on Smerdis's arm, she walked through the doors.

# 33

THE LONG table was heavily laden with rich delicacies from all over the land. Roast lamb, rice pilaf with almonds and raisins, spicy peppers, pickled turnips, curd cheese, olives, dates, figs, little cakes, curious fruits and nuts Jessica could not recognize and much wine. The centerpiece was a peacock, roasted but resplendent in its feathers. Jessica turned her head so she didn't have to look at it. The Red Lady sat at the head of the table. She said little to her daughter, but instead laughed and joked with the handsome captain of the royal army, her army. She did not seem so dangerous now, but Jessica knew she was just biding her time. Jessica watched the nobles of the palace refilling their plates and cups. Thin lips, wide lips, thick lips, rosebud lips all pouring food and drink into themselves before the following day's fast. A fast in honor of Kadi, the Horse God, on the day of the horse sacrifice. Jessica looked down at her hands.

Smerdis glanced at her. "Sister, why do you not eat?" he asked.

"I am not hungry, Brother," Jessica answered.

"Perhaps you have developed a taste for the mineral water and wheat biscuits they serve at Shabash Spa. I am sure we can fetch some for—"

"Let her be, Smerdis," Talliya said. "She has had a *long* journey." She smiled at Jessica. "And at least she will not grow plump like you."

The nobles laughed. Smerdis blushed. Then one woman, more a girl really, whose red hair curled about her head, said coyly, "I think his weight becomes him." She and Smerdis exchanged smiles.

"Yes, Adar, you would," the Red Lady said. "But you will think otherwise when all that flesh is lying atop your small frame."

The nobles laughed heartily and poked one another in the ribs. Jessica was shocked by the vulgarity and turned very red.

"Mother, dear, not in front of the young one," Smerdis said.

"Young? It is past time for her to wed. She has been stubborn, but I think she will soon consent. Next year grant that she may be bearing future princes of our empire."

Jessica winced.

"Who would you willingly take to your bed, Noura dear. Mabul here?" She nodded at the handsome army captain, whose arrogant smile suggested the match was already made. "Sarudin?" She looked at a thin, freckled youth who giggled. "Qajar, our newly appointed captain of the prison guard? She would be a rich reward for your loyalty, eh?"

"Qajar!" Jessica cried out and froze. He had stared into her face in the desert. What did he know then? What did he know now?

But the large, black-bearded, serious-faced man picked up his head from the contemplation of his wine and without looking at Jessica said, "That would be an honor, my queen."

"A pretty speech, do you not think?" the Red Lady said to Jessica.

She did not reply. The Red Lady looked curiously at her. "Now, now. He is comely enough. And he has brains. But if you like him not, there are others to choose from." She paused, eyes boring into Jessica's. Then, with a wave of her hand, she said, "I am tired. Pray continue without me if you wish." She rose and, followed by several ladies and Mabul, left.

Jessica sat silently, wondering, *what is she planning? What will she do to me? Well, there was only one way to find out.* She breathed deeply, gathering her courage. And as Smerdis called for more wine, she, being careful not to glance at Qajar, walked out of the room.

Jessica was not sure where Talliya's bed chamber was, so, behind a pillar, she watched the handmaidens scurry about the halls until she got a sense of the direction. Then she hurried that way. She reached a corridor with a number of doors. *Which one is it*, she wondered. A handmaiden came out of a room. "Oh, Princess Noura," she said. "I would not disturb your mother just now. She is—"

But Jessica brushed past her and into the room.

The first thing she noticed was a tunic on the floor. Then she heard the soft laughter.

"Mother, I would speak with you," she said loudly.

From behind the curtain, Mabul's tousled head emerged, then ducked back inside. "Your daughter has bad manners," he muttered.

Talliya's voice said, "Go now, Mabul."

Mabul grumbled and emerged, naked, from the bed.

Jessica averted her eyes.

Mabul picked up his tunic and threw it on. "I will return in one hour," he said. Then he grumbled, "Bad manners," again and left.

"Well, come here, Daughter," Talliya called.

Jessica parted the curtain.

The Red Lady lay pale and beautiful in her wide bed, her coverlet pulled modestly to her shoulders. "He is right. You do have bad manners. Is that the way you were taught to act in Wisconsin?"

Jessica started. The name of her homeland hit her in the stomach.

"There was no need to hurry. I would have sent for you soon," the Red Lady was saying.

What are you going to do to me, Jessica wanted to yell, but instead she blurted out, "You can't kill him."

The Red Lady smiled. "He is the Chosen One. He sits in the Sacred Chamber, preparing himself for the honor among all honors."

"That's your doing. You can 'unchoose' him."

"Perhaps." She smiled lazily. "If you give to me a certain tapestry."

She did not know. How was it possible she did not know? Peri had not come. Jessica still had hopes, but they were dimming. In that moment, she decided to stall for time. "First free him, then I will give you the tapestry."

"Do you think your thieving friend will find it?"

Jessica gave a strangled cry. "You do know! You do know!"

"Of course I know," Talliya said impatiently.

Jessica stood breathing hard. Finally, she said, "If you know that, then you must know where the tapestry is."

Talliya smiled her slow, curved smile. "Yes, I know where it is."

"Then why don't you take it?"

The Red Lady stopped smiling and looked intently at Jessica. Then, she shook her head and said, "Very well, Messenger. I shall explain yourself to you. I know where Gabdon is, but I cannot fetch him. When Tarkesh departed, the tapestry fell out of time—that Magus's doing, I am certain. Those who handled it then did not know its meaning. But you have discovered the tapestry and learned its secret—"

"He called to me. Gabdon called to me," Jessica murmured.

The Red Lady smiled. "Yes. I suppose you could phrase it that way. And now only you or one whom you delegate—may touch it. Only you—the Messenger—may give it away. Your thieving friend will bring the tapestry to your arms, and yours alone. It is then that you will make the choice of the person to whom you will give Gabdon. You will choose the Horsemaster."

Jessica gasped.

"You would have made it much easier on yourself and your friend had you given it to me in your own land. I gave you ample opportunity to do so. Now you are involved in a struggle you scarcely understand. However, I will do you a great kindness. For another Messenger, choosing the Horsemaster might have been quite difficult. He would have had to pray to the gods for insight, hear the testimony and supplications of the people, consult the maguses and priests until his head would whirl. I will do you the service of making your choice easy."

Jessica trembled with anger. So that was why Talliya had lured her to this place, had kept her alive, had not taken the tapestry from her when she was out in the desert. But Ashtar had not told her. Ashtar had lied, saying that Smerdis and his army would have seized Gabdon if they'd flown to the Imperial City.

How many other lies had he woven the way he had woven the tapestry? *A whole web of lies,* she thought. But why? What was Ashtar's stake in this struggle. *I want no part of his game. I don't care who gets the damn horse, or who becomes Horsemaster,* she wanted to scream. Then like a jagged tear of light, she recalled the strange dream of Gabdon she'd had in the cell. "You big lummox," she'd called him, as if he were a pet she loved very much. And she thought of Noura—hounded by the demons her mother had conjured up. But she was not Noura, not anymore. And she was not afraid of those demons.

Then, as if she had read Jessica's thoughts, the Red Lady spoke, "You are stronger than my daughter. You are past fear. That makes you a worthy adversary. But you have one great weakness. You love your friend. And so you will deliver Gabdon into my hands, or your dear friend Jack will be well honored tomorrow."

"No!" Jessica shouted. Her hand went to the dagger at her waist. She grasped the hilt and stood trembling, legs akimbo, wondering if she could seize Talliya's white throat.

The Red Lady's eyes grew hard. She raised her little finger. "Do not try, Messenger. Do not try."

Jessica felt a pain shoot into her hand. She cried out and her arm fell useless and quivering to her side.

The Red Lady said in a harsh voice, "Understand this. Give me the horse or your friend dies."

Jessica said nothing.

The Red Lady's voice softened, and that frightened Jessica even more. "Give me the horse, and my son will become shadoor, and I, Horsemaster. Together, he and I will rule this land. We will be the heart of power, the shining sun to which all will bow down, or be destroyed." As she spoke, her face became suffused with a dark glow, and her eyes flamed.

Then the Red Lady closed her eyes. And when she opened

them she was once more merely the beautiful, treacherous Talliya. "Now, daughter, go to your room."

"What if . . ." Jessica said hesitantly, ". . . what if Peri does not find the tapestry."

Talliya smiled once more. "She will find it. That one is clever and determined and will need only a little help from me. Now, good night."

Jessica spun on her heel and went quickly. But she did not go to her room. Instead, on impulse, she summoned Qajar. Let it all come out. *I have nothing to lose*, she thought grimly.

"Qajar at your service, my lady," he said, kneeling and kissing her hand. He did not seem ruffled or surprised at her summoning him.

"Qajar, do you not know me?"

He did not blink. "I know you, Most Beauteous Highness. You are Princess Noura."

Jessica did not correct him. Instead, she said, "Qajar, I wish to see Gamesh. Take me to him at once."

"Your highness, Gamesh is not a prisoner. He is a Chosen One. None can visit him."

"Qajar, I will pay you. I will do anything you wish. If you care about me—"

"Princess," Qajar said quietly, with embarrassment, "you know well the love I bear for you. But I cannot help you or Gamesh in this case. I am sorry."

"Oh, God," Jessica moaned. "It is hopeless."

Then Qajar said loudly, "But perhaps the princess would care to inspect the prisons instead. Now that the princess is of age, permission is granted. And there have been some renovations . . ."

"Oh, God," Jessica cried again.

He dropped his voice once more. "And there is a new prisoner the princess may find amusing."

His tone arrested her tears, and she looked up at him; but his face was inscrutable.

"All right," she said. "Let us go."

The hall was long and cold, as she knew it would be. Neither she nor Qajar spoke as they turned down the winding passages. Her hand traced the great friezes of tribute-bearers, processionals and battles carved in the stone walls.

At the end of a corridor stood two guards before a heavy iron-barred gate. They bowed to her and saluted Qajar, who saluted in return. Then he seized a torch and, unlocking the gate, led Jessica down into the earth. A rank smell assailed her, a smell all too familiar. Deeper. And the smell grew more intense. She covered her mouth and nose with her sleeve. Something caught her robe. She tried to shake it loose, but had to bend to free it. It was a chain to which was fastened what remained of a human leg.

She screamed.

Qajar rushed to her and kicked aside the bones. "It is only bone," he said. "We have long stopped dealing thus with prisoners. Shadoor Tarkesh saw to that. But Smerdis wants to reconsider the old ways."

"Beast," she muttered.

Qajar said nothing.

Deeper still. Jessica shuddered terribly, and her teeth chattered so she had to clamp her jaw hard to keep the noise from being heard. Groans in the darkness. Voices begging for mercy. And then they came to a torchlit corridor.

"The new cells," Qajar said, pointing here and there to small black cubicles, which revealed to the torch pallets of straw and crudely dug dung holes. "Do you approve of the renovations?"

Jessica did not know whether or not he was being sarcastic. She only knew she could not stand much more. "Where is the new prisoner?" she asked.

"This way."

At the end of the corridor was a cell with a door thrice bolted.

"Dangerous?" Jessica asked.

"Perhaps very dangerous. Thought to be a spy."

Qajar opened the door carefully.

The cell stank. The man in the corner lay on his back, his damaged arm heavy across his chest, his battered face swollen and discolored. He might have been dead or unconscious until through badly puffed lips he began to whistle a tune Jessica had heard many times before.

"Komar!" she cried, falling on her knees beside him.

In a voice cracked and strained, but still alive, he said, "Ah, little Vashti. We can once again do business."

# 34

HE ALLOWED Jessica's tears to bathe his hands. Softly, he said, "I was not sure that you could cry."

Her eyes still glistening, she answered, "I have been learning how to."

He tried to smile, but his lips burned, and he winced.

"We thought you were dead, Peri and I," Jessica said.

"Peri," he said tenderly. "My child is well?"

Jessica nodded.

"But Qajar tells me that Peri is not with you."

Jessica hesitated, then said, "She is looking for Moofta the donkey. I didn't want her to go, but she insisted."

"Ah yes, that donkey. What is so special about him?"

"I think I can answer that," Qajar said. "The tapestry is on his back, is it not?"

Jessica stared at him. So, he had recognized the tapestry, too. Slowly she nodded her head.

"Then I pray Peri succeeds." Looking intently at Jessica, Komar said, "So you are indeed the Messenger. The Noura who is not Noura."

"It is as Tarkesh dreamed and the Magus interpreted," Qajar said.

"You knew all along," Jessica said to Komar.

"No. I learned it but an hour ago from Qajar." He grimaced. "I do not like this business of dreams and maguses. Sheer superstition."

"Then how do *you* explain this girl?" Qajar asked.

"I do not have to explain her. I let her play her part."

Qajar laughed. "You are a very clever and a very stupid man, Komar."

Jessica turned to Komar. "So, Qajar has been your contact here. He is your spy who told you of Gamesh."

Komar smiled slightly.

"And you, Komar. You are not a thief."

"Oh, I am indeed a thief. And quite a good one, I might add," Komar answered, and he and Qajar laughed.

"All right, you are a thief. But you are also a spy. A spy for Tarkesh."

"Very good, little Vashti."

"Do they know you are a spy?"

"They suspect. That is why I am here and not lying dead on the streets of Medwar."

"And Qajar?"

"They may perhaps suspect him as well, although we take precautions. He was formerly liaison to Medwar and is, as you now know, Captain of the Prison Guards, where Talliya can keep watch over him. At any rate, they will do nothing. Yet. The battle for the throne will not take place for some days. If Peri can find the tapestry, there is hope. We will ride straight with it to Tarkesh."

"No!" Jessica snapped. "If the Red Lady does not receive the tapestry, she will kill Ja . . . Gamesh."

"You cannot save the boy. No one has ever freed a Chosen One," Qajar said gravely.

"I will save him. I will!"

Komar said gently, "He is a friend of yours. A Gamesh who is not Gamesh. But he cannot be saved. Moreover, it is a kingdom at stake and not simply a single life. You must remember that. I do not know whether I believe in this tapestry, this myth of the Horsemaster, but Tarkesh does. If the tapestry will make him take up the crown once again, then let him have the tapestry."

Jessica shut her eyes. She felt angry at this man who sat and told her that this land, this king she cared nothing for, was worth more than her friend's life. Then all of Komar's former treatment of her flooded her thoughts and she became angrier still. Her eyes snapped open and she was about to shout at Komar when his voice became brisk and businesslike: "Now listen. Listen well. Qajar must not be implicated in this. But as Noura is beloved of the people, you have the best chance. Still, you must be careful. Very careful. When you come to release me, you must come alone, and pray Queen Talliya will not divine your coming through the sorcery she is said to practice."

Jessica stared at him. "What are you talking about? Release you? Me?"

"You."

"How can I? What would I be doing in the prison if someone should see me?"

"Tomorrow there will be fewer guards on duty inside the palace. They will all be preparing for the Horse Sacrifice. You should not be seen. But if you are, you can say you dropped an earring somewhere in the cells last night while you were inspecting them and that you did not wish to trouble the guard to find it. The two prison guards will be incapacitated. I do not think they will be as clever as was Bahsboosa and fail to drink the generous amount of drugged wine Qajar will leave them."

Jessica still stared.

"Listen to me. Here is what you must do."

With a mixture of anger and hope, Jessica listened to Komar's words. "Come down while everyone is at the purifying bath. Unchain me and leave the cell door unlocked. A horse will be tethered by Qajar outside the West Gate." Then Komar repeated, "A kingdom is at stake and not merely a single life."

Jessica's anger flared bright once more. "No!" she cried out. "A life is a kingdom!" But then she said, "Listen to you with all your talk about lives and kingdoms. All you want to save is your own neck. A neck you think is worth more than Gamesh's. Well, it isn't. You don't mean anything to me. And neither does your precious kingdom!"

"You are right," Komar finally answered. "I mean nothing to you. There is little reason that I should. But this land, I think you have in you a love for it. A love for peace and freedom."

Jessica turned her head. There was truth in Komar's words, for Noura loved the land, and she and Noura were the same self. But she did not want to think about Noura. She ordered Qajar to lead her from the cell.

As they climbed the slippery steps, Qajar said to her, "Komar would not hold his life dear, Princess. But he can take a message to the king about the size of the troops here, the plan of attack. Gamesh cannot. And we cannot save him."

She shook her head furiously. "No! I don't believe you. Take me at once to the Sacred Chamber."

"Princess, I have told you—"

"Never mind then," she said sharply. "I will find it myself."

She rushed blindly up the steps and down the stone corridor. At the end, she came to a small wooden door she had not noticed before. She thrust it open and stepped into a courtyard. It was a beautiful place of ornamental trees, bright-hued flowers, goldfish pools. But she had no time to sit and admire the view. *Where*, she thought, slapping her hands against her cheeks, *where is the Sacred Chamber?* Then, as she stood gazing wildly about, a white-robed priest seemed to emerge from the ground and make his way down a promenade lined with pomegranate trees. She ran over to him and seized his arm. "Where is he? Where is the Chosen One?" she bellowed.

Startled, the priest looked in the direction of a stone slab from which he had come. Then he shook free of her arm and sped off.

"Jack!" she called, rushing to the slab. "Jack!"

She beat her hands against the stone until they bled.

But neither Jack nor the stone answered.

THE CORN already dry stubble. The leaves already as red and gold as a Chinese temple. And the air sharp with the coming of winter. A lone figure walked the field stopping here and there to look, part the browning grass and search. The figure neared. A woman, gaunt and disheveled.

She stood near her. Now so close they could touch.

"Mother," she called, "Mother, I am here."

The hollow-cheeked woman, eyes red from weeping, sleepless nights, did not embrace, did not see her, but kept walking, walking the dying field.

"Mother," she called again, "Mother."

But the figure was no more than a brown speck in the distance.

JESSICA woke with a sob, her arms reaching, her legs trying to run through stiff stalks. She fell from the bed and saw once again the cold stone walls of the palace around her. *Was that a dream? Only a dream,* she wondered, *Or is this the dream? When would a dream remain just a dream?*

She stood up, rubbed the elbow that had struck the hard floor and looked out the window. The sky was lightening. Then she remembered. Terrible dreams. Bleeding. Noura. Komar. And Jack. But no Peri. Why? Why? Why? The question beat in her head as it had before. Now here, alone, in her/Noura's room, she could scream it out. But the answer was always the same: Because. Because. Because. And the rest was silence.

A rap on the door.

She did not want to think of kingdoms. But there were all these individual lives counting on her.

Quickly she crossed to the door, put her mouth to the cool wood. "Yes," she said softly.

A snatch of a tune was Qajar's muffled reply.

"Yes," she said again.

Then she heard a girl's voice say, "Ah, out courting this morning, Qajar?"

Jessica held her breath.

"Maybe, Adar," Qajar answered.

"I wish you luck, then."

"And I you. You will be queen one day."

Adar laughed coyly. "Are you going to the baths?"

"Yes. May I accompany you?"

"You may," Adar said.

When their voices receded, Jessica breathed again. Then she flitted out the door like a small nighthawk.

Only when the heavy iron-barred portal was closed behind her would she be able to light the candle she held in the folds of her robes. All down the winding halls, she counted the paces to the door, as she had been told to do. One step. Another step. Once she saw a guard emerge from the shadow and look around, but she flattened herself against the wall, and he did not see her. At last, she reached the prison door. The two guards were indeed incapacitated, snoring and crumpled in drugged heaps at her feet. If anyone found them, he or she would suspect them of being drunk on duty. Grunting, Jessica tugged and heaved them away from the door. One stirred, grasped her hand in his and murmured, "Dear Lara." She pulled her hand free and, slipping off his heavy key ring, opened the lock and descended into the gloom.

She slipped twice before she felt it was safe to light the candle. Finally, she reached the cell. She chose the key Qajar had shown her and fitted it into the lock. The door opened noisily, and she froze.

"It is safe, little Vashti," came Komar's hoarse voice.

She entered, crossed to his side and knelt to unchain him.

His face was deeply cut and bleeding along the right cheek.

A great wave of pity washed over her. "They have hurt you again," she cried, and leaned over to wipe the blood with her sleeve.

"Do not!" Komar caught her arm. "You must leave no trace on yourself."

She dropped her hands helplessly.

"You are kind, little Vashti," he said quietly.

She gathered up the ring of keys. It was necessary to replace them so that if the guards were discovered, nothing would seem out of order. Then she turned to go. But, feeling the press of the scabbard she wore, she impulsively unhooked it and presented the gleaming hilt to Komar. "Use this well," she said.

He took the dagger, but said nothing.

Suddenly, she wanted desperately for him to survive. *A life is a kingdom*, she thought. And the ma-lat began to glow once more. "God speed," she said.

"Which god?" he asked wryly.

"Any one you like," she answered.

And they smiled at each other.

As she closed the door behind her, she heard him call softly, "I will return the dagger to you. Perhaps sooner than you think."

# 35

SHE WAS fingering a curious-looking musical instrument of Noura's—a psaltery perhaps?—when three handmaidens came to attend her. They led her to a tiled room with a deep bath in the center. She wondered why the bath was empty of people. Where were the other bathers? Then it occurred to her that there was probably one room for royalty, another for the nobles, and probably public baths for the rest of the populace. She let the handmaidens undress her, then help her down the steps and into the bath. She let them pat her dry with white cloths, then escort her back to her room. She let them smooth the night jessamine oil on the nape of her neck, the palms of her hands, then dress her in a purple robe and golden sandals and spin her hair in looped braids twined with golden chains.

They held a mirror before her, but she did not care to look. She dismissed them, but they refused to go, tittering as they explained that the princess knew they were her retinue for the great occasion, the most sacred of all the Sacred Days.

Then they waited—the maids whispering among themselves, Jessica sitting straight, eyes closed, nails biting into her scented palms. Still no Peri.

Within the great stone walls, Jessica could not hear the restless throng gathered to see a spectacle some revered, others merely enjoyed. Her mind whirled rapidly, but alighted nowhere. *What shall I do?* she thought. *What shall I do? Peri has not come.* How could she save him?

Then a faint tinkle of bells. The maids immediately stopped talking. The sound grew closer. And with it, a low droning chant.

Atma. Lasa. Kadi. Shadash.

Atma. Lasa. Kadi. Shadash.

Moosa, Moosa. Kadi, Kadi.

Shadash. Shadash.

In a file, the handmaidens stood waiting. Her head aching, Jessica rose slowly and walked stiffly through the open door, down the hall and out into the heat.

In honor of the horse god, Kadi, no one was to ride this day. And, humbled by the presence and power of this great god, all were to unveil their heads and faces. Thus, bare-headed and leading a gold-bedecked white horse, Smerdis led the procession up a sun-baked road lined by guards standing solemnly next to gloriously adorned horses. The guards held back throngs of worshippers. Smerdis glanced around furtively to see how many were admiring his piety and humility.

Resplendent in red-violet, an ironic smile on her beautiful lips, Talliya followed, head high, boldly waving to the crowd below.

Only Jessica stared straight ahead as she climbed the hill, the sun beating angrily at her neck and back.

They reached the crest and a small, sun-bleached pillared temple. On a pedestal was a flat stone carved with a man's head on a horse's body. Smerdis knelt before it and said loudly, automatically, "Blessed Kadi, grant us success in battle. Blessed Kadi, grant us success in peace. Shadash. Shadash. Shadash." Then, he kissed the stone, rose and turned to look at the valley below. Talliya, Jessica and several others followed his lead.

Below stretched a calm, shining lake. A white stone path led to its edge. White-robed priests walked the path, chanting and ringing bells. The crowd that covered the hill echoed their droning voices. Four priests set down a large golden palanquin and scattered petals over it. The chanting rose in fervor. Then a solitary priest led from the palanquin a naked, dark-headed boy who seemed to be swaying unsteadily.

"Jack!" Jessica gasped. Her hands shook.

The priest tugged the shaking boy into the water.

Silence. Then one thin voice chanted.

The water was up to Jack's waist. Then to his chest.

The priest held aloft a cup and poured it slowly over the boy's head. Red trickled down his face, upon his shoulders. He struck at the priest, but the holy man snapped out a big hand, gripped Jack's head and arm and began to push him under the water.

"NO!" Jessica screamed. "Let him go! Take me instead! Let me be the sacrifice!" She rushed forward.

"Hold her! Do not let her descend!" commanded Talliya, herself reaching for Jessica's robe.

The crowd began to press in. Mabul and two guards leaped out at Jessica.

But just then a small, dark woman stepped from the crowd. "Princess Noura," she said. "A gift."

The guards fell back.

Jessica spun around. The woman thrust a bundle into her arms. "I told you I would keep my word. I didn't think it was the donkey you really wanted," she said. Her scarf slipped from her head. It was Peri.

"Seize that woman!" Smerdis bellowed.

"Never mind the woman. Mabul, stay Noura!" Talliya called in a voice full of rage and surprise. She had not expected Jessica's reaction. And she did not want there to be any chance that Jessica would not "willingly" hand her the Horse God's son.

"Run, Vashti. Run!" Peri yelled.

Jessica froze, clutching the tapestry, bewildered by the voices pounding at her from all sides.

"Run!" Peri cried again, as the guards bore down on her. Jessica saw a sword slash, then Peri fall in a rain of blood.

"Oh, God," she sobbed, vaulting one-handed over the wall,

down the hillside into the confused crowd, with Mabul but a few yards behind her.

Jack and the priest were still struggling in the water.

"Stop it!" Jessica cried. "Let him go!" She plunged into the lake.

The priest did not hear. Mabul reached the lake's edge. Jessica held the tapestry high over her head. "Stop!"

Befuddled, Mabul halted. The priest loosed his grip. Jack's head bobbed to the surface of the water.

"Mother!" Jessica called. "Stop the ceremony, and I will give you the tapestry."

At the top of the hill, the crowd, murmuring questions, parted to reveal Talliya, arms crossed over her chest. She spoke calmly now. "Noura, I know not what you speak. Come up here and cease this sacrilegious behavior at once, or the guards will take you back to the palace."

Jessica's throat constricted. *Oh, no. I'm not going to lay this tapestry in your arms and let you kill Jack just the same,* she thought. Her hands gripped the tapestry tightly. Then an idea flashed through her mind. She began to sway gently to and fro. "Kadi!" she called. "Kadi!"

The murmur grew louder. Mabul inched forward. Jessica did not know if he would be able to force her back up the hill, but she didn't want to risk it. "Stop!" she ordered again, and again the captain halted. The priests did not move.

"Kadi. I see Kadi. His hair swirls in the wind. His hooves rake the sky. He is angry."

The voices of the people rose excitedly. "She has the vision." "Kadi. It is Kadi!" "The princess receives the god . . ." "The princess is heatstruck." "Listen to her. Listen!"

"He speaks," Jessica said. "He is angry."

Mabul faltered, but Talliya's angry voice stopped him from retreating. "I warn you, Noura. The heat has affected your brain. You only imagine you see the Horse God. Give that bundle of rags to Mabul and come back to your place."

"Mother! You displease the Horse God. He says the Chosen One is unwilling and you must stop the sacrifice else he will show you his displeasure. He will rive the sky with thunder, strike lightning off the horses' hooves . . ."

Some people began to moan, "Kadi! Kadi!" Others said, "Do not let him be displeased." Still others said, "She is mad. The princess is mad . . ."

"Priest Taboor, continue," commanded the Red Lady. "Mabul, don't let her near the boy."

"Mother, don't!" Jessica said, not knowing what she was going to do.

As the priest Taboor pushed Jack below the water once more, Mabul ran forward. Then, suddenly, a whirr, and he shrieked and stumbled, a gleaming silver dagger twitching in his back.

The priests screamed and fled as the horseman who had flung the knife galloped up the Sacred Path and into the lake, knocking down Taboor and seizing the drowning boy by the hair with his one good arm. In an instant the boy was before him on the horse.

More guards started to pour down the hill, but the frightened, shouting, running crowd impeded them.

"Hurry. Get on," Komar ordered Jessica.

She waded toward his horse.

"No, you will not." Mabul, dragging himself forward, choked out, and he sliced the horse's foreleg with his sword. Then, he fell lifeless into the water.

The horse crumpled, pitching Komar and Jack into the lake.

Jessica fought for her balance. Two guards had fought their way through the crowd and were heading into the lake. Jessica knew at once what she had to do.

Holding it high above the water, Jessica unrolled the tapestry and called the name. The air pulsed and shimmered. And Gabdon reared his head. For an instant, his eyes met Jessica's, and she felt such a communion with him she forgot where she was. Komar's voice brought her back to the lake.

"By the eyes of Padish, it is true!" he exclaimed. Then he pulled Jack up before him on the horse.

Jessica plucked the dagger from Mabul's back and scrambled onto Gabdon's back. The horse whinnied once and rose into the air, its human burdens clinging desperately to its back, as the guards futilely slashed their scimitars at his hooves.

And below Gabdon on the hill, Talliya, standing alone, shook her fists at the sky and cursed the universe.

# 36

"I MIGHT have known you'd bring us here," Jessica said to the horse, stroking his neck as he pawed the sand in front of Ashtar's stone house. "You know this place, don't you."

"If I had not seen this with my own eyes, I would not believe it," Komar said behind her.

She glanced back at him, smiling sadly, and then slid down from the horse. Jack was draped over Gabdon's back like a damp sack of flour. "Is he all right?" Jessica asked.

"He lives, but he needs food and rest," Komar answered. "Here, help him down."

Jessica caught Jack as Komar lowered him into her arms. Then, weak and sore, his arm hanging stiffly at his side, Komar dismounted and grasped Jack under his armpit. He and Jessica half-dragged, half-walked Jack into the shadow of the squat house.

They rested quietly for a moment. Then Jessica took a deep breath and knocked on the door. It swung open to her touch. "Ashtar!" she called.

There was no answer.

*That bastard,* Jessica cursed silently. *If I see him again!* But her thoughts broke off when she took in the scene before her. The floor of the house's single room was littered with fragments of pottery. The potter's wheel was broken in half. Chairs were smashed. Rugs lay in distorted heaps. Even the remaining loaf of moldy bread was ripped apart and scattered around an overturned table.

"The army of Smerdis has been here," Komar said after a long silence. "It must have happened some days ago. Come, let us pile some rugs over there and lay the boy on them."

Despite the heat, Jack was shivering fiercely. They used another rug as a blanket. Jessica smoothed the hair off his burning forehead.

"He should take willow leaves with wild onion. That will aid his fever. I will see if I can find some," Komar said and turned to go.

"Komar," Jessica stopped him. "About Peri, I didn't think they would . . ." She broke off as tears choked her throat.

"You are not to blame. She chose her own path. She did a great service, bringing the tapestry."

Jessica heard the bleakness in his voice. "You loved her very much," she said.

"Yes, I loved her, strange creature that she was."

"Oh Komar, I should not have let her go. Your child—"

"Enough! She is dead. The child also. Breast-beating cannot bring them back. Perhaps Peri now walks with Golgon in happiness. Perhaps she dwells in Zaboon. The only certainty is that she is dead. And because of her we are alive. If her death is not to be in vain, we must take this tapestry to Shadoor Tarkesh as soon as the boy awakes."

At the mention of Tarkesh, Jessica felt angry again. *He* was the one responsible for all this horror. If he hadn't left . . . Then Jack moaned, and Jessica turned to him once more.

"I will return shortly," Komar said. "Take care of Gabdon—whatever it is that you do with him—and bolt the door. I do not think anyone will come yet, but just in case."

He left, and she went out to the horse. He stood quietly, cropping a bit of tough grass. "My friend, I must make you vanish again," she said, "although I don't want to." Gabdon nodded his head as though he understood. "Oh, Gabdon, you're so beautiful. How could someone use you for evil?" she cried. But Gabdon didn't answer. Jessica made him disappear and went back inside.

"Jess, will you go to the dance with me?" Jack's voice, raspy from choking down water, rang out eerily in the decimated room.

Jessica sat down next to him and took his hand.

"I know it's just a stupid dance, but I could wear my motorcycle jacket and you . . ." His voice trailed off, and he shivered violently.

She wished she had some alcohol, something to bring his fever down. He was probably sick from shock or overexposure or something like that. All she knew about medicine was what she had learned in First Aid. *I only hope that Komar's willow bark or whatever he went to get works*, she thought.

"Jess!" Jack wailed.

"I'm here. I'm here," she said.

In a normal voice, he said, "So you will go to the dance with me?"

He had never asked her to a dance, but he must have wanted to. His words moved her to tears. *I've been so blind*, she thought. *That kiss! I didn't know he felt that way*. "Yes, I'll go with you," she said.

"Jess!" he cried out again and opened his eyes wide. Then slowly, as they focused on her, the fear left them. "Oh Jess," he said and gripped her hand. She smiled at him. He smiled back. "I won't tell your mother," he whispered.

She didn't know if he was joking or delirious. He sighed and fell into a shallow sleep still holding her hand.

Then there was a knock at the door. She disengaged herself and went over to it, then stood listening.

A whistled tune.

She opened the door.

Komar smiled at her. "We are in luck. I have found both willow leaves and wild onion. Now, if there is some water around this place, we can boil up an excellent medicine."

"What can we do for your arm?" Jessica asked.

"Nothing much. It will heal soon enough. There are no broken bones. But unfortunately it means I cannot massage your friend, which would make the medicine work faster.

Jessica found an unbroken pitcher of water on a high shelf, and Komar set about pounding the herbs in a wooden mortar that had rolled under a table. For a pestle, he used the hilt of Jessica's dagger. "The sun is so high, we can just leave this mixture outside to infuse," he said, handing her the knife, which she thrust back into the scabbard at her waist.

"How do you know so much about medicine?" she asked.

"A thief must know a little of everything. And that is what I know about everything—just a little."

He grinned at her, and she grinned back.

THEY HAD found and eaten some camhi nuts and dried dates, had slept and had dosed Jack twice with the medicine before the sun went down and the little house grew cooler.

"We cannot stay here much longer," Komar said. "They know of this house. It is not safe."

"We can't leave Jack. And he is not well enough to travel," Jessica answered.

"I have been thinking," Komar said slowly. "I could stay here and tend to him while you go with Gabdon to the shadoor. You can carry my message . . ."

"No. I will not leave Jack." Or you, she wanted to say, but the words would not come out.

"Oh, woman!" he shouted. "Do you want us all to die?"

She cringed. He had never shouted at her before. Nor called her a woman. Then she regained her composure. "If I leave you both here, you *will* die."

"The shadoor will come for us."

"But maybe not in time."

"If he is Horsemaster, he will not fail us." There was a queer hesitation in his voice.

"If? You still don't believe in the Horsemaster?" she asked.

He looked as if he wanted to swallow his words. "I do not know. He is shadoor, and that is enough for me." Then he waved his hand. "Besides, I am not sure I believe in a horsemaster."

"But you saw Gabdon yourself. You rode him!"

He just shrugged.

"Jess!" Jack called out.

She went over to him quickly and felt his forehead once again. "Oh, Komar, he's worse."

"His fever has yet to break. Give him more medicine."

"He looks so ill," Jessica said.

Komar crossed the room and peered at Jack. With his good hand he pressed gently at several places on Jack's body. Then his mouth became grim.

"What is it?" Jessica said, frightened.

"Bone sickness," Komar answered. "If we cannot make him cool, he may not live."

She did not know what bone sickness was, but it sounded terrible. She racked her brain for anything that could help Jack. And suddenly she remembered what Ashtar had done for her sunburn. "Palm fronds," she said.

Komar smiled broadly. "Clever one," he said and strode out the door.

Jessica gave Jack more medicine and waited for Komar to return.

When she heard his whistle, she threw open the door to find Komar with his arms full of wet palm fronds. Swiftly, he began to lay them over Jack's bare body. "It appears you too know something of healing. Now find another rug. We must cover him well. And we must give him medicine and water every hour."

Throughout the night they nursed Jack. He tossed and shivered and was delirious. When the sky became tinged with pink, he cried out once more. Jessica had fallen asleep next to him with her chin on her chest. She awoke with a start.

"Jess," he said. "I don't want to die."

"You won't. I won't let you."

"Please, water."

She held the jug to his lips. He drank noisily. "Good," he said. She felt his forehead. It was beaded with sweat. He sighed and sank into a deep sleep.

"Komar," Jessica called.

He was asleep. She called him again, and he roused himself from his place by the door and looked at Jack. Then, he smiled. "The fever has broken. He will recover. It is best now to let him sleep."

Joy rose in her like a wellspring. "Oh, thank God," she said, clasping Komar's hands. She wanted to dance and spin around the room. But she merely laughed and cried at the same time while Komar smiled at her. Then she tried to release her hands, but Komar held on tightly.

"Tell me," he said, "will you marry this boy?"

She felt herself blush. "I'm a little young to marry."

"No, little Vashti, you are of age. Peri and I were but sixteen when we married six years ago."

Her eyes widened in surprise. He was only twenty-two! She had thought him considerably older, not so much because of his looks, but his manner. Perhaps people matured faster in this country. Noura too had seemed older than her years. The thought of Noura made her ache, as though there was a hollow place inside her where something warm and good had been. Her anger flared once more, at Tarkesh, at Talliya, at Ashtar, at Komar, even at Peri for dying. It was huge, this anger; it threatened to fill the hollow place.

Komar was watching her. "Is it that you fear men?" he asked gently.

His question brought her back to the room, to him. She said slowly, "Sometimes, I like no one."

"Do you ever like me?"

She didn't answer.

He stood close to her, some large emotion causing his breath to come quick and shallow. "You have a mouth like Peri's," he said. There were tears in his eyes. Her anger died.

"Oh, Komar," she said. He bent his head and kissed her gently with his bruised lips. His arms came tightly around her. He smelled strange, musky and foreign, but it was a good smell. She put her arms around him. He kissed her again. The tears slid down his cheeks and onto her lips. He pulled away and turned his head in shame.

"What's wrong?" she asked.

"I . . . I . . . I have never cried be . . . before a woman," he stammered.

"It is a good thing to cry," she said. "That's something I've recently learned."

Komar looked at her and began to weep unrestrainedly.

And as he wept, Jessica felt his pain, her own pain, but through that pain, there came something deep and eternal in herself, in him, in Jack across the room. The hollow space inside her grew larger, emptier, and as a candle illuminates a dark room, it filled with light. She forgave Komar for all that he'd said and done to her, forgave her father for leaving, forgave her mother for the sorrow and bitterness that had caused her to hurt her only daughter. Then, Jessica felt that she belonged as much in this time as in her own. She felt they were all part of one time, of one Self. "Now I understand the ma-lat," she whispered.

And Ashtar entered the room.

# 37

JACK, KOMAR, the house itself seemed to fall away. Jessica faced her adversary. He was one person she could not forgive. "I said I would kill you if I ever saw you again," she said in a low, deadly voice, jerking at the scabbard at her waist.

"This then is your chance," Ashtar replied.

She held high the gleaming dagger.

Komar grabbed for her hand, but Ashtar said, "No, do not attempt to stop her. This is a scene to be played by two dreamers alone."

"Shut up!" Jessica snarled. "I'm tired of your dreams. With

those dreams you let my friend get captured, then made me come to this place and left me in the desert to die!"

Ashtar said nothing.

"I could have saved Jack a long time ago, but you lied to me. You said if we flew Gabdon to the palace, Smerdis and his army would seize him; but the truth was, I could have flown there, demanded Jack's release, and then handed over the horse. Talliya or Smerdis couldn't seize Gabdon without my consent because I'm the Messenger. And I would have given my consent. But you lied. And then you deserted me. Because of you, Peri was killed. And Komar almost died. And Noura . . . I don't know what's happened to Noura. You are an evil, lying . . ."

"Vashti, forbear." Komar turned to the Magus. "Is what she says true?"

"Let her finish," Ashtar answered imperturbably.

"You care for no one. No one. Well, now I have Jack and Gabdon with me, and you won't hurt them. You won't hurt anyone again."

With that, she charged at Ashtar. The knife flashed. Komar shouted, "No, Vashti!" But she thrust down the dagger. Its point quivered on Ashtar's breast. For a moment, she stared into the old man's brown, unflinching face. Then, a sound like a string breaking twanged in the air and, with a cry, she flung the knife away and smacked Ashtar's face once, twice, three times. She sank to her knees and began to sob bitterly, furiously.

Komar stood unmoving and unnerved, twisting his hands together until they turned red. And in his sleep, Jack moaned.

"There is a reason for everything," Ashtar said quietly, "even when there does not appear to be. It is true: I lied to you, and to Noura as well. But only because it was necessary. Would you not have trusted Talliya to release Jack then; as you did not trust her today? Without Gabdon, what bargaining power would you have had to protect yourself and your friend once you were 'free'? But you have, as you have just said, both Jack and Gabdon. You have . . ." He smiled a little, "all the aces."

"At what cost?" she hurled at him. "Peri is dead. Jack is very sick. And I . . . I . . ."

"There is no gain without loss," he interrupted quietly.

"Whose gain? Yours! Only yours!"

Ashtar said nothing, but Komar replied, "Vashti, that is not true. The gain is for all, for an entire kingdom. And, forgive me, but I believe it is also your gain. I . . . I have seen you open your heart, little Vashti; and that is abundance indeed."

Jessica turned her head from Komar and stared at the ground. Then, in an anguished voice, she cried, "Ashtar! Why did you desert me in the middle of a storm? Why did you leave me alone?"

"There are things one can learn only when one is alone," Ashtar said gently. "And you have learned much."

Then Jessica sat down and began to weep. Komar knelt beside her, his arm about her shoulders.

Abruptly, Ashtar began to speak in a matter-of-fact tone. "Daughter, you have been through much," he said. "I will release you of your calling. You are now free to go. Your friend will recover. Say the word, and you both shall return to Wisconsin, where your mother wastes away with worry."

Komar stiffened. And Jessica wiped her eyes and stared at the Magus. "You! You have the power to free me from being the Messenger?"

"I have the power."

"How can I . . . trust . . . such a traitor," she said.

"You can kill me if I do not keep my word."

"No," she said. "I cannot kill you."

"Then you must trust me."

Something in his voice compelled her to look deeply into his eyes.

"What about Gabdon? And Noura? She and I . . . we—"

Ashtar interrupted her. "I will return you to your land as I have promised. But you must have no more thoughts of Gabdon. As for Noura, you may think on her as a 'past life,' something to entertain your friends during cold winter evenings."

"Vashti, don't listen to him. Listen to me. The kingdom will fall if you do not help," Komar said urgently.

She did not answer him, but kept her eyes on Ashtar. "Why are you willing to send us back now?" she asked.

Ashtar was silent.

"Vashti, I beg of you." Komar cried out.

"Be still," Ashtar told him.

Jessica still stared at Ashtar. Then she asked, "Who will be the new Messenger?"

"You have asked enough questions, Jessica. Shall you and your friend prepare to return to the Middlewest?"

Jessica's head was whirling. *Gabdon, Noura, Tarkesh, Talliya. The ma-lat. I can leave now,* she thought. *We can leave, Jack and I. Then we will be safe. But Gabdon, Noura . . .*

"You did all this on purpose," she blurted out, "so I would be torn . . . so I would be forced to make my own decision."

Ashtar said nothing.

Agonized, she looked at Komar, whose eyes were soft and pleading, then at Jack peacefully asleep on the rugs. "Can you send him back alone?" she asked Ashtar.

"Yes."

She looked back at Komar, then cast her eyes upwards. "Help me," she whispered. "Help me."

Then she saw as in her dreams the corpse-strewn field, Smerdis's gloating face, Talliya's ironic smile, and proud Gabdon, an unwitting agent of destruction. And all of the feelings she'd tried to suppress rose, clear and full. She was the Messenger, and her message was to choose life over death. She had to deliver that message to a king and hope that he would deliver it to a world. The enormity and the simplicity of it left her speechless. Minutes passed. Finally, she turned to Ashtar. "If you will send Jack home, I will stay and finish my task."

"Kadi be praised!" Komar shouted. He rushed forward and flung his arms around her.

"Don't," she said, pulling away. "Not now."

"There is one thing," Ashtar said. "I can send the boy back only if he is willing to go."

"Oh no," Jessica said, knowing full well Jack would refuse to leave without her. And then she heard Jack say, "I won't go, Jess."

She whirled around. "You're awake!"

He smiled.

"How are you feeling?"

"Weak, but okay."

"Jack, I want you to go home," she said. "What I have to do, I'll do alone."

"Jess, if I hadn't twisted my ankle, none of this would've happened."

"That's not true. It would have happened anyway."

"I won't argue with you. But I didn't go through everything I did to leave now. I'm sticking with you, Jess, the way you stuck with me."

She threw her arms around him then, and did not notice that Komar had turned his head from them.

"Anyway, this has sure been a bigger adventure than Nebraska ever could've been," Jack said.

Jessica smiled and turned to Ashtar. "We will do what has to be done," she said formally.

Ashtar nodded.

For the first time, Jack noticed Komar and Ashtar. "You. I might have known," he said to the Magus. Komar introduced himself. Jack nodded and then asked, "Where do we go next, and when do we leave?"

"The Plains of Kashkeval. As soon as you are well," Komar said.

"I believe that I can, as you might say, 'speed up' that process," Ashtar said. "First this one." He touched Komar's hurt arm.

Komar jumped, then shook his arm. "By Bodar, it is healed!"

Then the Magus laid his hands on Jack's forehead. As Komar and Jessica watched, the sweat dried and the color came back to Jack's cheeks. "Now," said the Magus, "a good meal and we will be ready to depart."

"Some clothes might help, too," Jack said drily.

Ashtar laughed and found in a broken chest a pair of loose trousers and a tunic that had escaped being slashed by the marauders.

"Thanks," Jack said, springing to his feet and scrambling

into the clothes. Dressed, he turned to Jessica. "How do I look?"

"Lovely," she said.

He grinned. Then he leaned forward and touched her earrings. "Hey, these new?"

Her face darkened.

"Oh Jess. I . . . what have you gone through?"

She smiled grimly. "I'll tell you about it when there's time. Don't worry about me, now. Eat and get your strength back. Then I will summon Gabdon, and we will greet the shadoor."

They ate in silence. Komar seemed moody and impatient. Jack was busy with the food Ashtar kept readily supplying. Jessica watched them all. She was thinking that Ashtar could have healed Jack's ankle immediately when they were back in the old farmhouse in Wisconsin, and then none of this would have happened. She felt her anger rise again, but then she recalled what she had said to Jack: "It would have happened anyway." And she knew it was true.

They were almost finished with the meal when she heard a faint scuffling noise outside. "Ashtar," she whispered.

He looked up. "Komar," he said. A glittering scimitar flashed through the air and landed, hilt first, in Komar's hand just as the door cracked open and ten soldiers burst into the room.

"Kill all but the girl," a burly, red-bearded guard ordered.

Komar's sword slashed out. Two soldiers fell bleeding.

"NO!" Jessica screamed, brandishing her dagger, as she placed herself between two soldiers, and Jack. Out of the corner of her eye, she saw Ashtar evading a soldier's sword thrusts by disappearing and then reappearing in another place.

Jack pushed past Jessica. "Here," Komar shouted, retrieving a sword from one of the slain soldiers and handing it to him.

"Jack, watch out!" Jessica called, as a fair-haired man lunged at Jack's neck. Jack moved, and the sword grazed his forehead. "No, you don't!" Jessica screamed and thrust out her knife. She felt it thud into the soldier's back. The soldier sank to his knees, turning his face upwards. He was nearly as young as she. "Oh no," she moaned. "No." She backed away. Her eyes blurred over. Yells. Cries. Bodies everywhere, rushing through the door, about the room. Now there seemed to be twice as many men in the house. She felt sick. She turned her head and vomited. When she looked back, four men were gripped firmly by eight others, and seven lay on the blood-soaked floor, the flies already buzzing around them.

"Tie them up," the muscular captain was saying. "We will take them with us to the shadoor."

Komar stood breathing heavily. Jack was blinking away the blood that ran from his forehead into his eyes. And Ashtar was, once again, gone.

"Who are you?" Jessica asked.

"Shadoor Tarkesh's guards. The Blue Regiment." The captain bowed. "We have come to escort you to the shadoor. He wishes to see you. It seems we arrived just in time."

"I killed a man," Jessica said. Her voice rose. "I killed him." She knelt beside the young guard. He moaned.

"He is not dead. He is merely wounded."

But Jessica put her face in her hands. "It doesn't matter. I wanted him dead," she said.

"We will send a litter for him," the captain said. "Quickly, let us depart."

Jessica got the tapestry from under the pile of rugs that had served as Jack's bed. "I wanted him dead," she murmured again. "What kind of Messenger am I? Messenger of Life? That's a lie. A lie. Oh Ashtar, I am no Messenger. I'm a killer. Like the Red Lady."

"Jess, he would have killed one of us. You didn't stab him out of anger. You stabbed him in self-defense," Jack said.

But she did not reply.

"Come, we must go," the captain urged again.

Numb with shock, Jessica followed him outside into the rising sun. She no longer thought of summoning Gabdon. She thought of nothing at all.

The small group mounted the horses the regiment had brought.

"Aly-mai," called the captain. And they headed east for the Plains of Kashkeval.

# 38

THEY MOVED swiftly through the desert. The sun was high, but a breeze blew over the Rabala Mountains from the west, making morning travel bearable. Near noon they stopped, pitching light tents to protect them from the heat. For six hours they had not seen another soul.

"You may take rest now," the captain said. "We will stand guard."

Jessica crawled mechanically into a tent. She wanted to sleep, to blot out all memory. But she had barely closed her eyes when Jack slipped into the tent by her side.

"Do you mind?" he asked. "Would you rather be alone?"

She stared at the top of the tent.

"Do you want to talk?"

She did not move.

"Jess, listen to me. You struck that man in self-defense. You had to do it. This isn't Wisconsin, Jess. Everything's different here."

*Different.* The word reverberated in her head. It had no meaning.

"But," Jack was saying, "we're different and we're not different. When I was in that cell, I thought about a lot of stuff. I had plenty of time to think. First, I tried to make sense of what was happening. I mean, either I was crazy or this was weirder than any science fiction book I ever read. I thought about you and the questions you used to ask about magic and reincarnation and the story Ashtar told us and all sorts of things. But thinking didn't help. And then, I knew that the answers I wanted weren't there. There wasn't any making sense of what was happening. It was just . . . happening. There's something beyond thinking, Jess."

Jessica jerked upright, shuddering.

"What is it, Jess? Tell me. Tell me what happened to you. Tell me what we're looking for on the Plains of Kashkeval. You're my friend. I trust you and I'll go anywhere with you. But don't lock it all up inside and hurt yourself. Please." He touched her cheek.

She shuddered again. Then she became aware of his warm hand on her face. She looked into his eyes. The anger, the restlessness were no longer there. She rocked back and forth, wanting to cry out, to tell him all of it, but she couldn't, for the words would not come. "Hold me," she whispered. "Please hold me."

He gathered her into his arms. "Jess, my friend," he murmured, stroking her hair. Then they kissed. "Oh Jessie, Jessie." They lay down in a quiet embrace. She closed her eyes. If it were not for the heat, they might be in Wisconsin, she thought. But then she wondered if they would ever have gotten this close in Wisconsin.

*I wish I were a regular kid again,* she thought.

"Rest, Jess," Jack said, as if he'd heard her.

They fell asleep in the hot, still tent.

KOMAR AWOKE them some hours later. He entered the tent whistling, then stopped, gazing at the sleeping pair, their arms entwined about each other. He turned to leave, but Jessica sat up, rubbing her eyes. "Is it snowing?" she asked.

"Here? We are not so high in the mountains."

She furrowed her brow. "Who . . ." Then, she remembered and found her speech. "Is it time to go?" she asked.

He nodded stiffly. "I didn't mean to disturb you," he said gruffly.

She saw that he was distressed. She didn't know why, but it made her want to say something kind, to soothe him. All she could think of was, "Are you really only twenty-two?"

"Only?"

"In Wisconsin, you'd be considered pretty young."

"And where is Wisconsin?"

"In America. Where I come from."

"You do have a strange wit, Little Vashti," he said, shaking his head.

Jack stirred and threw his arm over Jessica's legs.

"Your lover awakes. Prepare to depart," Komar said and strode from the tent.

She reddened. "He's not my—"

But Jack sat up and cut off her words with a kiss. "Ummm," he sighed. "Oh, Jess." He leaned to kiss her again, but she stopped him.

"We have to go," she said. She suddenly felt removed, isolated from him. Sleep had soothed her only briefly, she had resolved nothing. *Why am I going to see Tarkesh?* she wondered. *How does he know about me? How can I be the Messenger? I am a killer, even if I didn't mean to be.* Without another word, she left the tent and mounted her horse.

The land grew flatter, and the sand mixed with soil. There were more grasses and yellow tuliplike flowers. Strange black stone columns rose here and there out of the ground.

"The Boldins," the captain said to Jessica. "Placed here many years ago by a people who no longer exist."

"What are they for?"

"We do not know," he answered.

Several times during the journey, Jack rode up beside her and tried to find out how she was feeling; but she only said, "I'm all right" and nothing more.

At nightfall, they came to an oasis. A number of slender trees dotted the edge of a pool. For a moment Jessica forgot herself. "This place is beautiful," she said.

Standing next to her, Komar, who had been silent and morose the entire afternoon, smiled suddenly. Then, stripping off his clothes, he yelled and ran down to the water. She watched his strong, muscled body arc silver in the moonlight, then plunge into the pool.

"Come on, Jess," Jack said, tugging off his pants. "It looks wonderful."

"Haven't you had enough water?" she said, wryly.

He grinned. "You know us Pisceans," he said and dashed in.

The soldiers were watching and laughing, but they made no move to join Jack and Komar.

"Come on in, Jess. It's terrific," Jack called. Abruptly, he rose in the air and tumbled down with a splash. Behind him, Komar trod water and laughed. Jack surfaced sputtering and charged at Komar. Soon the two were laughing and wrestling in the water.

Jessica smiled at them, but still felt estranged. The captain tapped her shoulder. "We will go to the other side if you wish to bathe."

She shook her head, thanked him and entered the trees.

Behind the slender trees were larger, older ones. They seemed to form a circle, to surround something. Jessica pushed through them. There, in the center, was a single tree, thick and gnarled, with a myriad of slender, drooping branches. Jessica had a sudden urge to embrace the tree, to clutch it tightly.

"The Tree of Memele," voice said.

She whirled around. It was the captain.

"I am sorry. I frightened you."

"No, it's all right. What did you call this?"

"The Tree of Memele. The child of Padish, God of Enlightenment, and Jamala, Goddess of Transformation. It is said that whoever spends the night in Memele's arms will be born anew by dawn."

"What does that mean?" she asked.

"I do not know." The captain smiled.

"Oh," she said, disappointed.

"Come rest yourself by the fire. After the horses have rested, we must depart once again. We must reach the shadoor's camp before dawn."

She nodded and followed him to the place where a fire was being built. Jack was slipping on his clothes once more. She sat down near him. Jack looked at her and asked gently, "Jess, they call you Messenger. What does it mean?"

"I must deliver Gabdon to the shadoor," she replied dully. "The horse that we . . . flew on?"

"Yes."

"Jess, isn't there something I can do?"

She shook her head. "Not until it's finished." She trembled slightly.

He wrapped a horse rug around her, but she still shook. They spoke no more until it was time to depart.

# 39

HOW CAN I tell of what has passed? The struggle was arduous. I was falling, falling, deep into the abyss of fear. All around me there was a roaring. But, above the roaring, as I fell, a small, still voice within me spoke. There is no fear outside the self, it said. Relinquish fear, and it will in turn relinquish you.

I reached for the voice. And then I was no longer plummeting, but floating. And I heard below me the Messenger in her pain. The Messenger who is myself. And self to self we spoke. She has relinquished her rage as I have relinquished my fear. And so we have both learned what the Magus wished us to learn. For it was he who taught us. He placed me here not to protect me, but to teach me. He left the Messenger alone so she too would understand. Together we are the Messenger. He says there is more to learn and tells me to fear not what will soon come. I tell him I am not afraid.

When there is an end to fear and rage, there is an end to killing. If the hearts of my people can be taught not to fear, not to lock anger inside, they too will join as one. This is what Gabdon taught my father. And it is what my father will teach the people when Gabdon is with him once again. Then, the Horsemaster and his daughter and their people will walk and speak together, free at last, in our blessed land. And that day will shine as no other, heralding the harmony of all things.

The Magus says I have learned much, but still he warns that I must not fear what will come. There is something he knows, but will not tell me. Some final test, perhaps, before I can be free. I do not know what it is. But I am not afraid. Truly, I am not afraid.

# 40

THEY SAW the fires long before they reached the encampment. The sun would not be rising for two or three hours more.

"There are lions in these parts. The fires keep them away," the captain explained to Jessica.

"I killed a lion once," said a tall, crooked-nosed soldier who was riding behind them.

"Stop boasting, Ahash," the soldier riding next to him said.

"I do not boast, Nadib. It was during the Maldean campaign. I was sleeping outdoors. Someone had stolen my tent. All I had was a blanket. I was sound asleep when this lion crept up and grabbed the blanket . . ."

"Then it took a look at your nose, laughed and ran away," his companion said.

The soldiers laughed. They were relaxing as they neared their shadoor and their familiar territory.

"Go ahead and laugh," Ahash jibed. "See what you do when a lion crawls into your bed."

"A lion crawls into my bed every night. I married her ten years ago," Nabib retorted.

The men laughed harder. Jessica could hear Jack, far to the

rear, laughing with them and realized he felt at home with these rough men.

They rode on, and then a cheer went up from the men. Before them the camp spread out like a strange city of tents and fires.

"Shabash! Shabash!" came the greetings from the soldiers who poured out of the tents.

Jessica dismounted, and her horse was immediately taken and tended by a boy who looked no older than ten or eleven. "Wait," Jessica said. Carefully, she took the tapestry from beneath the saddle rug. It was warm, and it cast a strange, silvery sheen. It seemed to her then that she heard Gabdon's whinny faint in the distance.

"Dear Gabdon, sweet Gabdon," she whispered. Suddenly, the dullness lifted from her. She felt overwhelmed with emotion —love for Jack, grief for Peri, compassion for Komar and an intense sadness that she would soon be parted forever from Gabdon.

"Golgon be praised!" came a shout. A roar of voices echoed the cry.

"Silence," said a soldier who appeared older than the rest. "The shadoor dreams."

The men grew quiet.

Jessica turned, as Komar came to her. When he saw the softness in her eyes, he reached out and laid his hand of top of hers. "Vashti, I wish to beg your pardon."

"What for?"

"I have been discourteous."

"Never mind that. You have reason. You've suffered a great loss."

"That is not the only reason I have been surly."

She waited for him to finish.

"Do not think me callous. I loved Peri with all my soul. But I cannot be alone. When my time of mourning has past, I would have you as my wife."

She found herself swallowing hard.

"Yet I know from what I have seen between you and the boy that such is not to be. He is a good boy. I like him. He will be a kind father to the many children you will bear. What I ask is that we may remain friends." The speech sounded so formal that Jessica knew he was serious and that he had carefully thought out what he was going to say to her.

"I'll always be your friend. As long as I'm here."

He caught the nuance. "Will you be leaving after you deliver the tapestry to the shadoor?"

"I hope so."

"I shall be sad to see you go."

"If I were older . . ." she murmured without realizing it.

"Yes?" he said.

She blushed and was happy the darkness hid her, for she was thinking of his soft lips, which had once kissed her, and wondering if she wouldn't have returned his kiss differently at another age. "If I were older, I'd know how to thank you for your proposal more gracefully," she said quickly.

"But you would still decline," he said, with a laugh.

"Yes, I'd still decline," she said, smiling.

Then Jack appeared and briefly touched her shoulder.

She turned to him.

"Are you all right?" he asked.

She nodded.

Ushered by two soldiers she, Jack and Komar threaded their way to a central pyre where two men were stirring a cauldron of something aromatic.

"You must be hungry," one said.

Jessica nodded. The soldier handed her a bowl of a thick lamb stew.

"Music!" one soldier cried.

"Music!" said another.

A husky young man reached for an instrument like the one Jessica had seen in Noura's room. Another man fetched a drum and still another a flute. They began to play a sweet, odd strain.

Jessica had to listen for a while before she realized it was Komar's song.

"Dance for us, Komar," a soldier called.

"Yes, yes," others agreed.

Jessica was pleasantly startled to see Komar jump to his feet,

throw his shirt to her and catch the little finger cymbals someone tossed him.

He danced slowly at first, snaking his arms in and out while
he tinged the cymbals, swaying his hips and undulating his
stomach.

"It's like a belly dance—only for a man," Jack whispered.

"Shhh," Jessica said as she watched Komar, open-mouthed.

The music got faster, and Komar began to dervish faster, too.
His feet beat a circle while his arms traced a complicated pattern
in the air. His body glistened with sweat.

At last the drum pattered a final crescendo and fell silent.
Komar sank to his knees, his arms outstretched before him flat
on the ground. When he rose, he was flushed and triumphant
and more handsome than ever. As he retrieved his shirt from
Jessica, he said, "That was the somora. Could you have danced
it for Bahsboosa?"

She laughed and asked, "How did you learn to dance like
that?"

"My father taught me. Did it please you?"

"It was great," Jack cut in. "A bit different from the stuff I do,
though."

"Oh, you too dance? Will you dance for us?"

"Sure," he shrugged. "If the musicians can play this." He
hummed a jig.

The musicians listened, then began to play, first haltingly,
then with more confidence.

Jack stood before the fire and, to Jessica's amazement, began
to do a fast, intricate jig. "Hey!" he shouted, clapping together
the heels of the boots Ashtar had given him.

When he finished, the men cheered and pounded on the
ground.

"How was that?" he asked.

"Very fine indeed," Komar said.

"I don't believe it," Jessica said. "I never knew you could do
that."

"There's lots of things I can do you don't know about."

"Where did *you* learn that?" she asked.

"From my mother," Jack replied, and winked at Komar.

They both laughed.

A strange honking sound interrupted them. Beyond the fire a man was blowing a ram's horn.

"The shadoor awakes," he announced.

"Shabash!" the soldiers shouted.

"He desires to see the Messenger."

Jessica rose to her feet. *Soon, it will be finished*, she thought. *Oh, Gabdon, I will miss you, my friend.*

The old soldier stepped forward to escort her and, as Jack moved to join her, said, "No, she must go alone."

He frowned, but stepped aside. "Come," Komar told him. "I will teach you to play sheshbesh."

Bearing the tapestry like a child, Jessica followed the soldier. They wended their way to a large tent. "I will wait out here," the soldier said.

She took a deep breath and entered.

The shadoor sat on a small carved seat. Near him was a table on which a single candle glowed. By the light of the candle, Jessica could see his lined, tired face, his deep-set eyes, kind but troubled. He did not speak, only stared at her.

She stared back, then, clearing her throat, she began, "Shadoor Tarkesh, I bring you—"

"Horsemaster," he said quietly. Then, louder, "Kadi be praised. It is the Horsemaster!" He sank to his knees before her and touched his forehead to the ground.

She backed away. "Get up. Please, get up. You are mistaken. I am the Messenger. You are the king and the Horsemaster. Get up, and accept Gabdon, or you will lose your kingdom and your wife will seize it."

But the shadoor remained kneeling. "Kadi himself spoke to me in my dream. My term is finished. It is now yours that begins. Take Gabdon. Face Talliya. Be strong and sure. And you will win. Now, I ask you to bless me, Horsemaster."

"No. You've gone mad! No!" Jessica shouted.

She heard Noura's voice cry with her, "It cannot be. Magus, it cannot be!"

"No!" Jessica shouted once more and ran from the tent. She rushed past the soldier and through the rest of the men, skirt-

ing the fires as she ran. Jack called her name, but she did not
turn. She grabbed the reins of the first horse she came to, flung
the tapestry on its back and threw herself on top of it. In terror,
she fled from the campground into the night.

# 41

"IT WOULD be better to kill me than to play cat and vole
with me. I trusted you, Magus. I accepted your explanations.
But now, now! How can the Messenger be Horsemaster? The
girl with my face? How can my father so believe it? I do not
understand. I do not believe you, standing before me with a
smile on your face. I do not believe you."

"In time out of time/When self by self are one . . ."

"You do not speak plain, Magus. You lie like the others."

"In time out of time/To ride the Horse God's son."

"I will not listen. I have learned not to fear, Magus. Did you
teach me not to fear only to show me how to hate?"

"In time out of time/The ma-lat lies within/Lose rage, lose
fear/ Grow strong, grow clear/ Then trust how it shall spin."

"How have you tricked my father? How have you forced him
to give up his office? How?"

"For the good of all/For the will of all/So must it be."

"And my mother? How did you fool her? Now there is no
Horsemaster, and my mother . . . my mother . . ."

"In time out of time/When self by self are one."

"Enough, Magus! Enough! You said those words when you
took me out of time. To keep me safe, you said. And then you
took that girl with my face out of time. And you . . . O Kadi!
The words—"

"Listen, Noura. Listen to the words."

"Oh, Magus. The words . . . I understand the words . . . And I am afraid."

"Listen to the ma-lat, and do not fear."

"Magus, do not leave me. Magus!"

"Listen . . ."

# 42

THE MOON had set. The sky was bright with stars, but they shed little light on the plains. Spurring the horse with her heels, Jessica rode frantically and blindly, unaware of time or place or threat of bodily harm from man or beast. Her body shivered, grew warm, then shivered again. Her mind tried to think, but she would not let it. Instead, she drove the horse faster until it was lathered with sweat.

Eventually, the exhausted animal slowed to a trot. "No, no, keep going," she commanded, but the horse refused to obey. Something familiar glimmered mirrorlike in the distance. The horse headed for it. Presently, its hooves plashed softly into cool, still water. It bowed its head and drank. Panting and trembling, she slid from the horse's back onto her knees. There was no sound save the horse lapping water slowly. She stretched out into the pool, submerging herself completely, then turning and floating on her back. She closed her eyes and let her mind float along with her body. She was dimly aware that the horse had left the pool and that she had drifted some distance from the edge, but she did not care. She did not know how long she floated before a voice said, "Jessica, listen. In time out of time/ When self by self are one . . ."

She looked up toward the dark grove of trees. "Who's calling me?" she asked. "Noura? Is it you?"

"In time out of time . . ." said the voice again.

"Noura? It is you, isn't it?" She emerged slowly from the water, her eyes fixed on the trees. From their center something reached out toward her, something quiet and concentrated, but strong and full, which seemed to flow straight into her heart. She knew then where she was. "The Tree of Memele," she said aloud. A slight breeze stirred the branches and she heard a thousand tinkling voices, merging, emerging. "One self. One ma-lat. Horsemaster, do what must be done."

"Noura? Noura?" she called.

Then, the single voice she'd heard before rose, bell-like, from the others. "Jessica," it said. "I am here." And Noura's image appeared before her. Holding the image steady, Jessica said, "You know my name."

"Yes, now I know your name."

"We are the same."

"Yes, the same."

"Are we Horsemaster?" Jessica asked.

But Noura had disappeared.

"Come back!" Jessica called.

But Noura did not.

For a long while, Jessica stood quietly, not even feeling the water dripping from her. Then she turned her head. The horse she'd ridden was standing by the edge of the pool. Without thinking, she glided over to it, took the tapestry from the animal's back and walked silently through the grove to the Tree of Memele.

The branches spread above and around her like a dark waterfall. She touched the bark of the tree briefly. Then she unrolled the tapestry until it lay gleaming beneath the tree. Pressing her hand against her heart, she called, "Gabdon!"

The horse appeared at her side. She laid her hand against his forehead. "My friend, my big lummox," she said. A white light lit up the inside of her skull. Noura was there, the image of her spirit sharply etched against the white. She began to speak.

"I was a seeker. I prayed over and over to the gods to know the ma-lat. 'The shadoor, the soldier, the dancer, the thief, all have, all are the ma-lat," the Magus said. But I did not understand. 'The eagle, the tiger, the rabbit, the flea, all have, all are the ma-lat,' he said. But I did not see. 'The lily, the willow, the lichen, the wheat, all have, all are the ma-lat,' he told me. Still I was blind. But then you came. And then I began to see. Now, the remaining shreds of the blindfold have slipped from my eyes. At last I too understand the ma-lat."

The leaves of the tree rustled softly in agreement.

"Noura, am I, are we, Horsemaster?" Jessica asked once again.

"Yes," said Noura. "Together, self by self, we . . . you . . . I am Horsemaster."

From the opening of her heart, Jessica knew it was the only answer, the only truth.

Then a wind rose, tearing suddenly through the long limbs of the Tree of Memele. Jessica felt herself soaring into space, black and vast and endless. But she was not frightened. A white light streamed from her, light upon light until she was the light itself. And all the while, Noura remained before her, and the light poured from her as well. They reached out their arms to one another, felt themselves merge and blend, self by self, soul by soul, until they were one. Then that one tumbled gently through space until she found herself next to Gabdon, her hand on his forehead. But this time, resplendent in a many-colored patchwork robe, Ashtar was there.

"When Noura was born, I saw as great a spirit in her as rested in her father. She will be the next Horsemaster, I thought. And I prayed to Kadi that it be so. But Kadi told me the next Horsemaster would be born of pain and struggle, with neither his blessing nor his curse. For such was the agreement of the gods of which I spoke to you, Jessica, some time ago. When Talliya turned to the left-hand path, I saw that struggle take shape. Kadi entrusted me to weave the tapestry of his son and gave me the power to take it out of time, but he gave me no power to choose the Horsemaster or determine the outcome of the struggle. It was I alone who decided to help Noura all I could. Then Tarkesh left. He did not leave out of weakness. He departed, knowing that the fierce contest was at hand and that from that contest the next Horsemaster would emerge. He could have no part in the choice, but had he remained he could have been used by his wife to evil ends. Yes, I lied to both of you about that. I lied so that Noura, who was not yet strong enough, who was weak and afraid, might become a match for her formidable opponent. I lied so that you, Jessica, would perhaps forgive your own father his leaving. You have learned from Noura as she has learned from you. Together, you are whole."

Then she smiled sadly at him. "I'm not sure I'm glad to have paid the cost of that learning."

He did not reply to that. Instead, he said "The Red Lady waits. She has grown even stronger. The struggle is not over. The final contest is yet to be held. You will need to be surer than you have ever been. If there is a seed of fear, of rage, of doubt in you, she will find it and feed it. Are you certain you are ready to face her?"

She said nothing for a moment, only gazed up at the sky and saw that it would soon be dawn. Then she said, "I am ready."

Ashtar nodded twice and held out his hands in the formal, supplicating gesture he'd waited long to perform. "Will you come now, Horsemaster, to heal your kingdom? Will you come to teach as you have learned?"

"Yes," she said. "Yes, I will come."

The Magus raised his hands until the palms faced him, then he placed them together and bowed until his forehead touched his knees. "Blessed be," he whispered.

"Blessed be," the Horsemaster answered.

# 43

IN THE bright dawn, the stony battlefield spread out gray and pale yellow, waiting to run red. Smerdis's men, specks in the distance, were advancing slowly. They outnumbered Tarkesh's army two to one. And although Tarkesh was thought to be a better tactitian, Smerdis had his mother and her magical arts on his side as well as numbers. It was with great gravity that the shadoor led his troops to the plain. He did not want to fight, but he did not intend to be deposed as shadoor, to sit by and watch his wife and son destroy all he had worked to build. Though he had fled his kingdom, he had fled to insure a strong Horsemaster, not a wicked one. He prayed that his daughter would return with Gabdon, but there was no sign of her nor of the Magus. "She will come," he told a grieving Komar before their departure from the camp. "She must come." Jack too grieved. He couldn't believe that Jessica had deserted him. But he didn't know what had happened. He was desperately trying to figure out what he could do when Komar rode up beside him.

"We ride now," Komar said. "Do you ride with us?"

"Do I have a choice?" Jack answered. He wanted to ask what they had done with Jessica, but knew he would get no answer he would understand.

"Yes. You may stay here."

"And do what? Wait until I'm captured and stuck in a cell again? I can't do that. I'd rather go looking for Jess."

"Those are not a soldier's words," Qajar growled at him.

"I'm not a soldier," Jack answered.

Qajar gripped the hilt of his sword.

"Hold, Qajar. Ride ahead. We will join you."

Scowling, Qajar trotted off.

Komar faced Jack and spoke urgently, "Listen to me. You will undo all if you try to find your friend. It will be better for you to ride with us and pray for her return."

Jack stared at him angrily, but Komar's face was so pained, he understood in a flash that this man had fallen in love with Jessica and prayed too for her return. His anger drained. "All right. I'll come with you," he said simply.

"Then let us go," was all Komar replied.

BELOW THE BLUFF, astride their horses, the shadoor and his usurper faced one another. At Smerdis's side was the blacksmith, Gamesh's father, and a red-bearded soldier. At Tarkesh's side, Qajar and Komar, dark and silent, were tensely listening. Jack stayed with the other men, but his eyes strayed to the bluff. He had agreed to wait, but he was not sure he'd be able to keep his word.

Red-faced and sweating, Smerdis spoke. "Father, I have no love of war, nor does my beloved mother. But your reign as shadoor is finished. You have become old and inept. Give up the crown willingly, and no blood shall be spilled."

The shadoor drew himself erect. He looked now as formidable as he had once been, and his voice rang out clearly in the still air. "That my son, I will never do."

"There is no way for you to 'will,' for you have lost the will of the people. You are outflanked, my father, outflanked and out-stripped. But you can yet abdicate with honor."

"Honor," Tarkesh said quietly. "You do not know the meaning of honor."

Smerdis turned redder still, and the blacksmith and the red-beard stirred angrily.

"Father, I give you one last chance."

The shadoor glanced up toward the top of the bluff, then back at his son. "Sound your battle cry," he said. Then, to Qajar, "Go call the men to arms."

"So be it." Smerdis spat. He and his men turned and rode away.

Tarkesh gazed after him, his face white and pinched. "The judgment of Kadi upon my head," he murmured.

Komar and Qajar looked at one another and shook their heads.

ON THE PLAINS of Kashkeval, the two armies faced one another. Their banners waved lazily in the warm breeze. Slowly, to the fore of each battalion, rode a soldier holding a long copper horn. Each blew a sharp, staccato blast, then turned and rode back to the ranks. Next Smerdis and Tarkesh each rode foreward, right hand raised, poised to give the signal. Behind them, the men strained forward, hands on their sword hilts. Someone had given Jack a sword. He looked at it with disgust and anger. He was going to die. To die without seeing Jessica ever again, without even attempting to find her. He looked up at the bluff again. If I could get up there, maybe I could escape. It was worth a try. He began to nudge his horse away from the others.

"Glory to Smerdis," cried out the blacksmith.

"Glory to Tarkesh!" answered Komar.

The shadoor and his son stared across the plains at one another. Then, simultaneously, they cried, "Aly-redon" and whipped their hands down through the air.

"Ai-ee," shouted the men and charged forward.

The air began to ring with the cries of men and the clash of metal on metal.

Jack's horse, confused between the charge and the direction Jack was urging her, reared up, throwing her rider to the ground. He rolled clear of the hooves and stumbled to his feet.

On all sides men were rushing madly at one another, hacking and slicing. Groans and screams and the sickly sweet scent of blood filled the air. Jack, dazed, was holding his sword before him. It was broken. He did not know how it came to be so.

It was then, at the top of the bluff, that the girl appeared, small, slim and shining. "Behold!" she called, holding up the tapestry.

The men froze, turning only their heads and gazing at her.

Carefully, the girl unfurled the tapestry and called the horse's name.

The air pulsed and shimmered. In the absolute silence rang out the sound of hooves against stone. And then, Gabdon stood at her side.

A sigh rippled through both armies, and it was like the whisper of the wind in the Tree of Memele.

The girl mounted Gabdon and rode slowly down the bluff through the mass of men, calling Jack's name. At last, she came to Jack. He was still confused. "My friend, are you all right?" she asked.

"Jess? Where were you? What—"

"Hush. It's all right now. Come sit behind me."

But a silken voice stopped him from moving, "My daughter, you are mad." And from the frozen throng, the Red Lady walked, unruffled, and unscathed, delicately picking her way over the wounded. She faced the girl, who dismounted and stood quiet and erect.

"You think you have vanquished me. Ah, you have learned nothing. See, you still care more for this boy than for this kingdom. And you still fear me." Then, she crossed her arms over her chest and began to hum. A dense gray mist surrounded her, crackling as if she were a forcefield. And through the mist, the Red Lady held out her hand. "I have grown stronger. And you are Messenger no longer. Now you are my opponent, and I shall crush you. Gabdon!"

At once, he trotted to her side. The mist disappeared. The men gasped. But the girl was silent.

"Who is now Horsemaster?" the Red Lady said. Her eyes blazed with a red light.

The girl held her gaze steady and said nothing.

Then the Red Lady's face warped into a mass of snakes.

Smerdis screamed; but his howl was lost among the cries of his soldiers. Some tried to run or cover their eyes, but they could not. And from Tarkesh came the cry, "No, Talliya! No!."

"Look on!" the Red Lady commanded. The snakes hissed and writhed, then slid to the ground and disappeared. In their place was a nest of scorpions, poisoned barbs upraised.

"For the love of Kadi, stop!" Tarkesh bellowed.

The screaming of Smerdis and the men rose in pitch.

But still the girl stood and watched. From the corner of her eye, she saw a movement. With an enormous effort, Jack had managed to take several steps toward the Red Lady. He held aloft his broken sword, aiming the edge at her. "Watch . . . out . . . Jess," he said.

But the Red Lady raised her hand, and Jack dropped the sword with a cry of pain. The girl felt Jack's love for her fill her heart, joining the compassion and strength already there. "Mother! Look into Gabdon's eyes. He comes to heal you."

The force of her words made the Red Lady turn and look into the horse's eyes. And as she stared, her chest began to heave and her hands to tremble. "No!" she cried. She tore her eyes away and faced the girl once more. But now, her face was blank except for a dark light flickering in a dark sphere, and in this her daughter could see the depths of Talliya's fear and guilt and pain. "Mother," she said, "I love you. And I entreat you. Do not turn from Gabdon and from me."

The voice came out twisted in pain. "Daughter, you do not love me. You have never loved me. You loved your father. But you did not love me. Nor did your father."

"Mother, my father adored you, as once I thought you adored him."

"I loved him as no woman has loved. I wanted . . . I wanted . . ."

"Mother, what did you want?"

"Power for him. Only for him. But he did not care."

"You bent the power, Mother."

"I would not have bent it if . . ."

"If?"

The answer was a cry that cleaved the Horsemaster's heart. "If he had loved me!" The dark light flickered. And deep within it, the girl saw, bent in upon itself, a torn, twisted soul, but a soul nonetheless. "No, you Daughter of Za-ka, no!" the Red Lady screamed, her own face reforming once more.

"Mother, listen to me. I love you, Mother. I love you even now. You can no longer hurt me. But you will destroy yourself. Listen."

The Red Lady did not heed her, but threw her arms to the sky and chanted, "Ak-za, ma-lat, pak-za, doomor!"

A wind whipped the air. Suddenly, the soldiers were able to move. They stumbled against one another, fell on the ground or cowered behind rocks and scrubby bushes, covering their eyes and mouths with their arms. Black clouds thundered in. A bolt of lightning rent the sky.

"Mother, listen!"

"Ak-za, ma-lat, pak-za, doomor!" the Red Lady shrieked.

And on the horizon, a mass, like a black sandstorm, appeared, rolling rapidly towards them.

With a whinny, Gabdon clopped softly over to the girl and nuzzled her hand.

"Ak-za, ma-lat, pak-za, doomor!"

The mass raced toward the Red Lady, then hovered at the edge of the melee. The Red Lady pointed at her daughter. "Razoon!" she commanded. From out of the mass came a huge hand, gray and cold. It stretched out toward the girl.

"Mother, Mother, don't!" she said. But the Red Lady shouted, "Razoon!" once more. The girl turned and faced the demon hand. Standing perfectly still, she whispered something, and bands of light began to encircle her from the crown of her head to her feet.

The hand reached out further, its fingers nearly touching the bands of light. Then, abruptly, it curved, and, with a sucking noise, bore down on the Red Lady. The shadoor's wife screamed, and both she and the hand vanished from sight.

The light faded from around the girl. There was silence as she wept for the Red Lady. Then, she raised her head and looked out over the throng to Jack. He was frightened and confused. She smiled and held out her arms to him. He ran to her and let her cradle him. Then the men began to mutter and shake, knocking against each other. Smerdis cried out and ran forward to the spot where his mother had stood.

"Seize him," he bellowed and pointed at Tarkesh.

It was Komar who leaped at the shadoor's son.

"Do not let our lord be taken," cried the blacksmith, on foot, driving ahead, sword drawn. "Come. Fight me, you dog!"

"It will be my pleasure to slit your throat," Komar answered.

They lunged at one another, as soldiers in both armies shouted and drew their swords.

The girl took a deep breath and listened. Although she heard no words, she understood all. The ma-lat flowed through and around her in an ellipse of light. Mounting Gabdon, she rode in between Komar and the blacksmith and grasped each one's sword blade in her hands. Her hands did not bleed. In a voice filled with radiant power, she commanded, "Hold!"

The clamor ceased, and the men looked to the girl mounted on the white-starred chestnut horse.

"Have you all not yet learned? Will war bring peace? Will death bring life? My brother, look to your father. He has lost his queen, as you have lost your mother. Komar, you have also lost your wife. Will killing this man bring her back?" And the light poured from the girl out into the crowd, into their hearts and minds. "I am the Horsemaster. And this is my teaching. Henceforth, in this land there shall be no more battles. You shall look to the ma-lat in each of you, and you shall find peace." Then, over Gabdon's neck, she broke the two swords. The horse tossed his head and snorted. She held the shining pieces aloft. And to the surprise of all, herself included, they stiffened and turned gray, then brown, and then burst into green leaf.

"Horsemaster!" The murmur swept through the assembly. "Horsemaster!" The men brandished their swords aloft and every one of them turned into an olive branch.

"Horsemaster," Tarkesh said, kneeling. "Daughter. Forgive me for allowing you to suffer alone."

"I forgive you."

Komar stepped forward and knelt. There were tears in his eyes. "Can you forgive all my past injustices to you?"

"They were forgiven long ago."

Jack stared in wonder. "Jessica? Are you still Jessica?"

She smiled at him. "For you, always," she said.

Then the Horsemaster turned her head. The Magus was by her side. "Have I done well, Ashtar?" she asked.

"Yes, my child, you have done well," he said.

She stroked Gabdon's neck. "I think it's time for Jessica and Jack to go home, isn't it?"

"Yes," said the Magus. "It is time." He lifted his hands, touched thumb and index finger and pointed the other three fingers at a huge Boldin. It shuddered and rumbled. But the men did not notice. They were rejoicing. The shadoor held his son in his arms, as the young man wept. Only two were watching the rock as it quaked—Jack and Komar.

The boulder lifted and rolled harmlessly to the side. From beneath rose a boy very like Jack. In his arms he carried a girl, limp and lifeless, with Jessica's face. She wore the royal robes of a princess.

"Oh God, it's me!" Jack cried out.

But the Horsemaster knew otherwise. "Gamesh!" she shouted with joy. "Gamesh!"

# 44

GAMESH LAID Noura's body on the ground. "You will bring her back?" he asked the Magus.

"I will bring her back," Ashtar replied.

Then Gamesh looked at Jack. "I tried once to speak with you, but my words could not pierce the veil."

Jack said nothing, only nodded.

The Magus held up Noura's ring. The blue stone glinted richly in the sunlight. Then, carefully putting one foot before the other, Ashtar walked around the princess, drawing with her ring a circle of light like a misty shield. When he was finished, he turned to the Horsemaster. "All is ready."

"A moment," she said, and went to Komar, who knelt before her, the tears still streaming down his cheeks.

"Princess ... Horsemaster ... I ..."

"Vashti."

"Vashti . . . I do not understand . . . Noura who is not Noura . . ."

"Yes. But Noura will be with you as herself once more and soon." She knelt down beside him, and, turning his face to hers, kissed his mouth. "That is from Vashti. Remember her as one who cared for you."

"Vashti, must you go?"

"Yes, I must go."

"I have lost all I have loved."

"No. You can't lose the love itself. Promise me you will remember."

"I will remember. Always."

Then, she rose and went to Gabdon. She looked into his eyes. "Goodbye, big lummox," she said, "I'll miss you. But Noura will treat you well."

Gabdon snorted gently as if to say, "I too will miss you."

She wanted to linger, but she knew it would only make the parting more painful, so she turned to the Magus. "I am ready," she said.

He nodded. "Close your eyes . . ."

She thought the separation would hurt, but it did not. As gently as a skein of yarn unraveling, there was a little pulling, a little snip, and she was Jessica alone once more. She opened her eyes. The body in the shield of light began to stir, then stand.

Noura stepped through the light and faced Jessica. This time they had no words to say. They stretched out their hands until their fingertips touched, then turned from each other.

Gamesh led the princess, now Horsemaster, before her people. Smerdis and Tarkesh and their men knelt before her.

Jack took Jessica's hand.

"Come," said Ashtar. They followed him as he led them up the bluff. Jessica put her hand to her mouth, feeling the touch of Komar's lips as Noura's soft voice floated up, "I will walk with you as Horsemaster in this land, so that together we may learn the way of peace."

"It is done. She will rule wisely and well," Ashtar said.

Jessica nodded.

"And now, link hands, for your own circle of time and place beckons: your work here is finished."

Jessica and Jack obeyed. Then Jessica said, "Ashtar, one question.

"Will I remember?"

For a moment Ashtar did not speak. Then he said. "Your mind will want to forget, but you must not let it. You must hold fast to your remembrance and your knowledge. It will be hard, but you are strong; and if you succeed, you will become stronger with each passing year."

She smiled at him, but her eyes were filled with tears.

Ashtar began to chant, and Jessica and Jack, thinking of green rolling fields and brick houses, joined in with him.

Like the hum of a dragonfly in her ear, Jessica heard the Magus say, "Go my child, be a Horsemaster in your own land. Teach as you have been taught. Listen to the ma-lat. And never cease to learn."

"Oh, Ashtar," she called and reached for his hand. She felt a touch light as a dry leaf.

And then the world spun, went gray-brown, green and white, and flung them forward into a familiar circle of time and space.

# 45

THE SNOW blew lazily, powdering the frozen ground and bare trees with a fine coating. They stood shivering in their thin jeans in front of the old farmhouse, shivering and enjoying the sensation.

"It's beautiful," Jessica said, her hair slowly becoming white. "Beautiful."

"I never thought I would like the cold so much," Jack responded.

"It started here, Jack," Jessica said.

"No, Jess, it started way before here."

She smiled. "You know what I mean."

He smiled back.

"Let's go. It's a long walk."

"Walk, my foot. We'll hitch."

THE FRIENDLY driver chattered away, blithely unconcerned with the fact that his two passengers said little. "Gonna be a real cold one. You two better dress warmer next time you go for a Thanksgiving hike."

"Thanksgiving!" Jessica exclaimed.

"Yep. Did you forget? Ha-ha." The driver chuckled.

They didn't answer.

"No school for you two, right?"

"Yes, that's right," Jack answered.

"You must be glad about that."

"Yes."

"Well, here we are. Brown Deer Road. Say, I know it's

Thanksgiving and I usually don't work today, but do either of your mothers need brushes."

"No. No brushes," Jack said quickly.

"Oh, okay. Maybe some other time."

"Yes. Try us around Christmas," Jessica said, stifling a laugh.

"Alrighty. Enjoy your vacation."

Silently, they watched the car drive away. Then, Jack said, "I'll come with you, Jess."

"You don't have to," she said.

"No, but I want to. I don't know how much of this we can explain, but—" He stopped.

She smiled at him. "Even now I'm not sure I believe it. Except for these." She touched her ears still ringed with the ornate circles.

"It happened though."

"Yes. It happened."

"He said we will want to forget. But we have to remember."

"We will. We'll remember."

Linking hands, they turned onto the slate path, slippery with snow, cutting through the wide lawn to the porch of Jessica's house.

THE TABLE was set for three. Candles. A small turkey. Dishes of cranberry sauce, mashed potatoes, carrots, green beans sat there barely touched. Jessica quietly opened the door. She and Jack silently approached the dining room and looked in. The worn woman was asking, "Won't you have some more?" to the uncomfortable, heavy-jowled man and his thin, nervous wife.

"No, thank you," he said.

"This is very kind of you," his wife added.

The woman sighed, and a heavy tear rolled down her cheek. "But it won't bring them back, will it?"

"Let's face it. They're gone," the man said.

His wife began to cry.

"Mother," Jessica said quietly.

"Mom, Dad," Jack said.

The three adults looked at the doorway.

"Jack! Son!" cried his parents simultaneously, rising to their feet.

Jessica's mother also rose, dropping her napkin and knocking over a water glass. "Jessica? Oh my God." She stumbled over to her daughter and embraced her.

"Where did you go? What were you trying to prove?" Jack's father demanded.

"It's a long story," Jack answered. "We were hitching to Nebraska and got as far as South Dakota. We worked on a ranch. It was okay. We didn't get into any trouble; but after a while, we wanted to come back." It was the story he had decided to tell his parents. "They wouldn't believe the truth," he had said to Jessica.

But his father said. "There were police looking for you on all the highways. We heard from some cops who thought they saw a couple of kids fitting your description. But they must have been drunk because they told some garbled nonsense about a flying horse."

Jessica and Jack said nothing.

Then, Jack's mother said, "It doesn't matter where you were. You're home now. And you won't run off again, will you?"

"No, Mom, I won't."

Then, she straightened up, and, with more vigor than Jack or anyone had ever seen her show, she looked right at her husband and said, "And he's not going to be sent away from home either." She hugged her son.

Jack's father lowered his head and blew his nose into his handkerchief.

Jessica's mother was still crying and holding her daughter. Jessica held on tightly. Finally, her mother turned to the others and said in a shaky voice, "It's a real Thanksgiving this year. Let's celebrate it. I'll get more plates."

Jack and Jessica smiled at one another. His mother and father nodded. Then they all sat down around the candlelit table and began to eat.

\* \* \*

AFTERWARDS, when Jack and his family had left, Jessica and her mother faced each other over the candles. "Jessica." Her mother searched her sunburned face. "Can you tell me what really happened? I know you weren't in South Dakota. I had such dreams. And a little while ago, a pain at my throat like a hand closing around it . . ." Her voice trailed off.

"I hope I can. Sometime," Jessica answered.

Holding hands, they went to the window and looked out at the glistening lawn.

"It's going to be a cold winter," her mother said.

"I don't mind. Do you?"

"No, not now." She paused. "I thought I'd lost you forever. I couldn't bear it—not after losing your . . . your . . . father. I even wrote to him about you at the last place he was supposed to be." The pain in her voice was unmistakable.

"Did he answer?" Jessica asked gently.

"No. He never did."

"Momma." She laid her head against her mother's cheek. "Momma. He's gone. Gone for good. He doesn't love either of us."

"No, he doesn't."

"But Momma, I love you. And I know you love me."

Without a word, her mother kissed her, and the two wept quietly together, while the white snow fell soft and silent.